Henry Steelman is starting from scratch.

She entered a side door, anxious to finally discover the mystery of cooking. Lots of people at the bank thought it was relaxing and even listed it as a hobby on their job applications.

Henry smiled. "Imagine doing something for fun that can be done just as well at a fast-food restaurant."

She rounded the corner to the kitchen. Examining the class roster outside was a tall, well-built man in a stylish gray suit.

Henry sucked in her breath. *My, my!*. Was he really that good-looking or had she suddenly reopened her eyes to the male species?

As if he felt her stare, he turned and flashed her a bright smile. "Ah. There you are. I was afraid I was late."

"Excuse me?" Had they met before and arranged to meet here? Surely she would have remembered.

The stranger gestured at the kitchen, where younger men and women nervously examined pots and cooking utensils. "I was afraid they'd be mostly college age, and I was right. Everybody else has checked off their names on the list, but I see there's another man signed up."

"We're supposed to sign in?" Henry stepped closer to the sheet.

"Aren't you Vera Fabbish, the instructor?"

"The instructor?" Henry laughed, fishing a pen from her purse. "No, I'm afraid I'm one of the lowly students."

"But the only other name on the list is—"

"Henry Steelman." She checked off her name with a flourish then extended her hand. "Don't feel bad. People always mistake the name for a man's."

He looked her up and down. Bewildered, he shook her hand. "What's a *woman* doing at a beginner's cooking class?"

JANE ORCUTT lives in Texas with her husband and two sons. She was a 1996 finalist for Romance Writers of America's Golden Heart award for best inspirational romance. *The Fruit of her Hands* is Jane's first book published with **Heartsong Presents**.

Don't miss out on any of our super romances. Write to us at the following address for information on our newest releases and club information.

Heartsong Presents Readers' Service
P.O. Box 719
Uhrichsville, OH 44683

The Fruit of Her Hands

Jane Orcutt

Heartsong Presents

To Kay Wiesmann and Carol Thomson—excellent wives,
mothers, and sisters.

To Bill, Colin, and Sam for their love and patience.

Thank You, God, for the promise of Isaiah 42:3.

A note from the Author:
I love to hear from my readers! You may write to me at
the following address: **Jane Orcutt**
                              Author Relations
                              P.O. Box 719
                              Uhrichsville, OH 44683

ISBN 1-57748-011-2

THE FRUIT OF HER HANDS

Cover illustration by Jeanne Brandt.

PRINTED IN THE U.S.A.

one

"Whatever happened to peanut butter in a kid's lunch, anyway?"

Grumbling, Henry Steelman jerked open cupboard doors, searching through the cans. Brian had asked for chicken salad, and chicken salad it would be.

A quick glance at the gold wristwatch elicited a groan. Tardiness was frowned on at the bank, and Clayton Fitzhugh probably wouldn't accept lunch making as a valid excuse, even from one of his officers.

"Aha!" Eager fingers gripped a can emblazoned with a smiling cartoon hen. "Gotcha, Miss Clucky! Now, if I can just find the mayonnaise. . ."

Thirteen-year-old Brian slammed past the kitchen's swinging door. "Can you put some egg in it? Last time it was awful! Just chicken and mayonnaise!"

"Sorry." Henry fumbled with the can opener. "You know I'm not used to cooking."

He laughed. "I never thought of chicken salad as *cooking* before."

Henry winced. How embarrassing. The kid was right, of course. No doubt he was even more skeptical about what was on the menu for dinner.

The opener slipped off the can and clattered to the floor. Exasperated, Henry sighed. "Can't you just buy your lunch?"

"Sure." Brian pushed back through the doorway. "But we used to get good lunches before."

Before. Henry leaned against a counter. Yes, before they'd all had it better. Better food, a cleaner house, the kids' homework done on time. . .

Henry smiled wistfully. "Spouses just shouldn't die."

When Leslie was alive, things had been different. Mornings had been pleasant affairs with lightly seasoned poached eggs, crisp turkey bacon, and exactly one and a half mugs of coffee stirred with a dollop of cream. Leslie knew all the family's favorite foods and all the daily, quirky schedules.

Les never would have forgotten that Brian had soccer practice on Tuesday afternoon or that Cindy's ballet lesson finished at five o'clock rather than five-thirty. Les would have known that Brian liked eggs in his chicken salad sandwich. Or how to make chicken salad in the first place.

Henry stared at Miss Clucky, feeling a smile rise at the hen's absurdity. Life did go on. They'd muddle through, somehow. Pastor Reynolds counseled it would take a long time to get over the shock.

Henry snapped a banana from the stalk, then absent-mindedly reached in the knife drawer. Just a quick breakfast today. A big business lunch was always nourishing.

The banana peeled easily, and Henry chopped the banana into three neat sections. With the last stroke, the knife cut into flesh. Blood oozed from the wound and dripped over the pale yellow fruit.

"Can't *anything* go right around this house?" Tears sprang from weary eyes, smearing expensive mascara.

Eight-year-old Cindy burst into the kitchen, and her

eyes widened with shock. "Mom, you're bleeding!"

Henry smiled weakly, reaching for a paper towel. She moistened it under water and wrapped her injured finger. "I'll be all right, honey." She drew herself up on three-inch-high Italian heels, shaking shoulder-length brown curls with resolution.

❧

Henry entered the main suite of First Houston Bank's Personal Trust Department at exactly one minute after eight, walking with purpose and confidence. *This* was her world, the one where she fit and moved with ease. She'd known ever since she was a little girl that she wanted to work in a big office building just like her daddy. She'd worked hard to get where she was today. Les's death hadn't left the family financially destitute, but now more than ever, Henry needed to advance in her career. A vice presidency would mean greater security.

"Mornin', Henry." Joe Preston leaned out of his office. "You watch the football game last night?"

"Sure did," Henry said, suppressing a grimace. She'd meant to clean the bathtubs, but an interesting fumble had occurred in the middle of the second quarter to turn the tide of the game.

"Good morning, Mrs. Steelman." Louise, Henry's secretary, held out several envelopes. "These came for you late yesterday."

"Thank you. Anything exciting happen after I left early?"

"I'm afraid not." Louise smiled. "How was your daughter's ballet class?"

Henry pretended to study the mail. "It seems the class was over at five and not five-thirty like I thought.

I not only missed seeing her rehearse, but Madame Corkly was ready to lock up by the time I got there. Cindy was pretty upset with me."

"That's a shame. You know, my mom keeps telling me that the kids are only young once. I hate when I miss something exciting like Tommy's first steps."

Henry shrugged, sifting through the mail. "Why don't you stay home with him, then?"

Louise lowered her eyes. "I'd love to but I have to work. We couldn't make it on Mark's salary alone. Maybe when he's through getting his master's degree. . ."

She trailed off and a smile reappeared. "I'm lucky I have my mom to watch Tommy. Someday I'll be home with him. It'd be nice if I had a house husband who—"

The mail stilled in Henry's hands and she froze, waiting for the inevitable backpedaling.

"Oh, Mrs. Steelman, I'm sorry. I forgot your husband . . .well, that is, that he. . ." She bit her lip.

Henry smiled. Usually the pussyfooting annoyed her but she knew the young woman well enough to recognize sincerity. "I don't mind talking about him, Louise. Really."

"I. . .I'm sorry. I thought it wasn't polite to mention someone who's dead."

"I wish somebody *would* mention him. Les was the world's best husband, and I still want everybody to know it." Henry sighed. "But until I see him in heaven, I've got all kinds of work here to do on earth."

"Oh. . .oh. . .yes, ma'am." Louise backed toward her desk. "I didn't mean to keep you."

Henry smiled a farewell and passed the bustling cubicles of the clerical pool on her way to her own small office. She closed the door behind her for a few moments of privacy. Already exhausted, she plopped down in the swivel leather chair as though it were the end of the day instead of the beginning. She had barely stowed away her purse before someone rapped on her door then opened it without invitation.

Clayton Fitzhugh, manager of the bank's personal trust department, stormed in. A stern-looking man in his late fifties, he ran the department as a captain ran a ship. And right now Henry felt his exasperation like a pointed sword at her back, forcing her to walk the plank.

"You were late again, Mrs. Steelman. Our hours start at—"

"Eight o'clock sharp. I'm sorry, Mr. Fitzhugh, it's just that—"

Clayton braced his palms against her desk. "You've been here how many months, Mrs. Steelman?"

"Eight, sir."

"And in what capacity were you hired?"

"Trust officer, sir." Henry had the absurd inclination to stand and click her heels.

"And what's the next step on the promotional ladder for you?"

"Vice president, sir."

Clayton straightened. "Do you think it's wise to waltz in late every day? Or to leave early? Do you see the other officers doing this?"

"No, sir, but they're all men. They have wives who take care of—"

"No excuse!"

Henry jumped back in her chair and the casters squeaked.

"I will *not* give you special privileges because of your gender. Either be here on time or don't be here at all!"

"But, sir, my work is always done on time. And our customers always have good things to say about—"

"No excuse!" Clayton whirled and stomped out. Arms full of manila folders, Louise slipped through the doorway just before the door banged shut.

Henry exhaled a whoosh of air. "I guess you heard that."

Louise nodded, solemn.

Henry sighed. "I ought to be able to do all this. Other women do. It's a good thing I'm not ready to date."

"How will you know when it's time?"

"I've been wondering that myself, but I haven't met any man I like well enough. Brian and Cindy have made friends since we moved to Houston, and I think it's time for me to do the same. Outside of my sister, Mary Alice, I don't even know many other women."

"What about your church?"

Henry grinned. "As a matter of fact, I signed up to attend a cooking class there. My church is in between the University of Houston and Rice, so we offer basic cooking classes for students. My first lesson is tonight."

"You mean. . .you really don't know how to cook?"

"I can barely boil water," Henry said cheerfully. "But lately my kids have looked a little thin, so I figured it was time to do something about it."

"Well. . .good luck," Louise said skeptically, pushing the folders across the desk.

Henry took the first one off the top and grinned. "Thanks. I'll need it."

two

"Sorry to leave you with the cleanup," Henry said, waving at the pots and dishes stacked in the sink. "But if I don't make tracks, I'll never get to the church by seven-thirty."

Mary Alice eyed the mess and smiled breezily. "Don't worry about a few dishes, sis. Just be sure to get there on time. I'm for anything that will help you learn how to cook."

"So are the kids." Henry grinned. "One bite of my meat loaf, and Brian clutched his stomach as though he were reenacting the stabbing of Julius Caesar. I don't think he was half-kidding, either."

Mary Alice headed her toward the door. "You'd better hurry. It's already seven, and you never know about downtown traffic."

Henry slung her purse strap over her shoulder and checked herself in the hallway mirror for suit wrinkles. Hopefully no one would notice that spot of tomato sauce on her lapel. Maybe if she—

"Go!" Mary Alice gave her a more persistent shove and opened the door. "Have a good time!"

"I will. The kids are already doing their homework, and I told them they could have a snack later. Don't forget to—"

The door banged shut, cutting off her last instruction. "Guess she's tired of looking out for us," Henry said.

She shrugged, unlocking her late-model four-door car.

As she drove from the suburbs to downtown Houston, Henry thought about her younger sister. Mary Alice had always enjoyed baking and cleaning house. No one in the family was surprised when she and her high school sweetheart married and immediately started a family.

Henry and Les had also married straight out of high school, but they had Brian just after they both graduated from college. Eight months pregnant, Henry had waddled across the stage to accept her business diploma.

She eased the car into one of the few available spaces in the church parking lot. That was nothing unusual. The church had a variety of evening classes for members and the community. Henry had already volunteered to help organize a food distribution program as soon as things were more settled at home.

She entered a side door, anxious to finally discover the mystery of cooking. Lots of people at the bank thought it was relaxing and even listed it as a hobby on their job applications.

Henry smiled. "Imagine doing something for fun that can be done just as well at a fast-food restaurant."

She rounded the corner to the kitchen. Examining the class roster outside was a tall, well-built man in a stylish gray suit.

Henry sucked in her breath. *My, My!* Was he really that good looking or had she suddenly reopened her eyes to the male species?

As if he felt her stare, he turned and flashed her a bright smile. "Ah. There you are. I was afraid I was late."

"Excuse me?" Had they met before and arranged to meet here? Surely she would have remembered.

The stranger gestured at the kitchen, where younger men and women nervously examined pots and cooking utensils. "I was afraid they'd be mostly college age, and I was right. Everybody else has checked off their names on the list, but I see there's another man signed up."

"We're supposed to sign in?" Henry stepped closer to the sheet.

"Aren't you Vera Fabbish, the instructor?"

"The instructor?" Henry laughed, fishing a pen from her purse. "No, I'm afraid I'm one of the lowly students."

"But the only other name on the list is—"

"Henry Steelman." She checked off her name with a flourish then extended her hand. "Don't feel bad. People always mistake the name for a man's."

He looked her up and down. Bewildered, he shook her hand. "What's a *woman* doing at a beginner's cooking class?"

"Same thing you are, I guess," she said cheerfully. "Trying to learn how to master the basics."

"*Master?* You must be at least thirty years old. Are you telling me you don't know how to cook?"

His remark about her age deflated her usual good nature. "Thanks for the compliment. I'm thirty-five."

"Look, Miss Steelman. Just because—"

"It's *Mrs.* Steelman. And no, I can't cook. Good-bye."

Henry turned into the kitchen, flashing fake smiles at the other students as she strode to the farthest end of the room.

Rude man! Why were some people surprised when a woman didn't know how to cook? She certainly wouldn't insult him if he didn't know how to change a tire!

"Hello, hello!" a female voice boomed. "What a crowd

tonight! You all flatter me with your presence."

Henry turned in time to see a corpulent, older woman in a multicolored flower muumuu enter the kitchen. A hot pink ribbon swept up her gray-streaked dark hair, and her warm eyes flitted from student to student as she nodded her greetings. In her left hand she gripped the class roster. The other hand was in constant motion— shaking hands, touching a shoulder, ruffling the hair of a preteen. She called everyone by name, and everyone returned her greeting with enthusiasm.

"Tom. . .Paula. . .good to see young newlyweds. You can't live on love alone, you know. Even the first year of marriage. Ha-ha! Andrew. . .Steve. . .Mark. . ."

She stopped at Henry. "I don't believe I've met you, dear. I'm Vera Fabbish. Are you here with one of your children?"

Henry's smile felt weighted. "No. I'm here on my own."

Vera leaned closer. "Good for you!" she whispered. "Don't ever be afraid to try something new." She winked and moved on to the next student.

While Vera finished her rounds, Henry noticed that Rude Man had skulked inside and loitered near the door.

"At least I had the courage to march right on in," she muttered.

Vera took her place at the head of the stainless steel island, where she had a view of the entire class. "Who's here to learn how to cook?"

Silence. Everyone looked at each other, perplexed at the obvious question.

"Good." Vera beamed, leaning her palms on the counter. "Because this class isn't about cooking. It's about taking care of the ones we love and even those we don't. And sometimes," she grinned mischievously, "it's about just plain taking care of ourselves."

She straightened. "We all have to eat, right? Some would argue that it's not how fancy the food but how it's served. I agree. Jesus fed thousands of people with bread and fish, and I'll bet it was the best meal they ever ate."

"Did I wander into Pastor Reynolds' Bible study by mistake?" someone cracked.

The room laughed, Vera right along with it. "All right. I'll get off my soapbox. Let's start with a few questions so I can get a general idea of the class's experience. Who can bake a turkey they'd be willing to feed their in-laws?"

A few hands raised, Henry's and Rude Man's not among them.

"All right. Who can bake a casserole. . .of any kind . . .that they'd be willing to feed their immediate family?"

More hands shot in the air. Henry glanced away. Her eyes met then darted from Rude Man's, whose hand stayed at his side.

"Who can bake a potato, even in a microwave oven?"

All hands raised except Henry's and Rude Man's.

"Make a grilled cheese sandwich?" Vera said hopefully.

With a confident smile, Rude Man raised his hand. Henry studied the tomato spot on her lapel.

Vera looked at her. "Dear, can you butter bread?"

"Yes."

"And slice cheese?"

"Of course!"

"And you do know how to operate a stove top?"

The others burst into laughter. Henry managed a grin, wondering how much longer she could endure being the butt of the class's jokes. Even Rude Man laughed, the nerve of him!

"Quiet down, everybody," Vera said, motioning with her hands. "The point is that all of us have the skills to cook. We just don't always know how to put them together to come up with something palatable. And that's why we're here. Like everything else in life, cooking takes practice. Which we'll do here away from your homes, prying eyes, and disapproving taste buds."

A few people shot Henry apologetic glances, which she returned with a smile. Rude Man studied his nails. The corners of his mouth twitched.

"For this class we'll work in teams of two," Vera said. "The goal is to encourage each other, not to tear down. If I hear one word of criticism, the offender will be forced to eat his own cooking!"

Her hot pink hair ribbon dangled over her ear as she squinted at the roster. "When I call your name, pair up along the counter here."

"Just like Noah's Ark," someone mumbled.

"Andrew and Shelly. . .Tom and Grace. . ."

Henry noticed she rattled names off the list, not making any effort to match people who had obviously come to class together.

"Henry Steelman and. . ." Mrs. Fabbish squinted. "I can't read the signature, but the initials are R. M."

Henry stopped in midstride to the counter. *Rude Man?* It couldn't be! Wouldn't that be a joke!

"I guess that's me," a deep voice said behind her.

Henry turned, heart sinking at the sight of the handsome man's—*Rude Man's*—smirk. He took his place beside her, extending a hand. "I never got to introduce myself. I'm Rick Montgomery."

"Mr. Montgomery," she said coolly, clasping his hand in her best business handshake. His eyes crinkled at the corners.

"Good. That's settled." Vera beamed at the paired-off class like a proud matchmaker. "The first order of business is aprons. Then I'll arrange you all in your places and we'll start with breaking eggs."

Someone groaned. "That's not cooking!"

"Young man," Vera said sternly, "there's an art to cracking an egg and telling if it's fresh or not. Good cooks need to know both. Shelly, please pass out the aprons. Meanwhile, let's take our places."

Vera spaced the couples evenly down the counter, side by side. Henry and Rick didn't even look at each other as they dutifully tied large canvas aprons behind their necks and waists.

Henry finally glanced up. She'd seen Les wear an apron a thousand times, but never over a business suit. She laughed.

"What's so funny?" Rick smiled faintly.

"You! Instead of the Galloping Gourmet, you look more like the Bounding Businessman!"

Rick's smile deepened. "You don't look too realistic yourself with your own suit. Are you in cosmetics sales or something?"

Henry's laughter died, and she straightened. "I'm a bank officer."

Rick raised his eyebrows.

Vera set a crock of eggs between each couple and an empty bowl in front of each student. "Most people make their mistake by whacking the egg against the bowl like they're opening a can of biscuits. Tap the egg's circumference on the table, like this, then ease it open over the bowl."

The egg's contents dropped into the bowl without a sound. Vera set aside the shell. "Now each of *you* try," she said. "And remember, no wisecracks!"

Rick grinned at Henry. "Ladies first?"

"Age before beauty?"

He laughed. "I'm thirty-seven. You've got me there." He reached for an egg.

Henry noticed how tan his hands looked. His long, slender fingers curled around the egg in an oddly protective gesture and rolled it delicately in the curve of his palm. He had the hands of an artist or a musician, smooth and expressive.

He gently tapped the egg against the counter.

"It works!" Rick peered at the egg in his bowl then proudly held up the even shell halves. "And not a speck of eggshell in the bowl."

He rested his hand near Henry's bowl. "Come on, it's your turn."

Unnerved, she picked up an egg. Her fingers shook as she tried to tap the egg on the counter. She carefully lifted the broken egg over her bowl.

Halfway there, the egg slipped from her grasp and plopped right on the back of his hand. She stared at the mess, mortified.

"Hey!" Rick swiped at the sticky blob with his apron.

Henry snapped to life. "I'm sorry! Let me help." She grabbed the hem of her own apron and knocked over his bowl. The puddle of goo headed in a dangerous stream for the edge of the counter, but Rick caught it with his apron. He rubbed the sticky edges together, then glanced up, smiling. "Yuck."

"Yuck is right," Henry said, embarrassed. "I am so sorry."

He propped an elbow on the counter and studied her. "It's okay, Henry. I've cleaned up my share of my own messes. Before she died, my wife always said I couldn't crack an egg. I guess you and I have that in common."

Henry forced a crooked smile. "Actually, we have a lot more. I'm a widow."

He stared at her a moment, then cleared his throat. "I'm sorry about how rude I was earlier. Will you let me make it up to you by going out for coffee with me after class?"

"Well. . ." She cocked her head, pretending to consider. "I really don't know you that well, Mr. Montgomery."

"What do you want to know? I'm a Houston native, I like golf, I—"

"Oh, save it for your coffee later!" Vera broke in. "Right now you're supposed to be cracking eggs." She turned to Henry. "He's been a member of this church all his life and that's recommendation enough, dear. You'll go with him, won't you?"

Henry held up her hands in mock surrender. "I guess I don't have a choice now!"

Vera's gaze traveled from the counter's gooey remains to their soiled aprons. "Not if you want to pass my class," she said dryly.

three

"You're not going to insist on driving, are you?" Rick said as they walked out to the parking lot. "If you handle a car the way you crack eggs, I'd better make sure my insurance premium is paid up."

"No." Henry recognized his teasing tone. "This was your idea, so you're in charge."

Rick unlocked the passenger door of a maroon minivan in dire need of a wash. Henry squinted in the dim light then smiled. Someone had traced a heart in the grime on the passenger door.

The inside, however, was surprisingly clean, much tidier than the usual clutter Brian and Cindy managed to leave behind. The upholstery and dashboard gleamed as if straight from the sales lot. Henry sniffed, imagining she smelled fresh leather. Rick probably used the vehicle for professional purposes.

"New car?" she said as he started the engine and backed out.

"Last year. I bought it right after my wife died."

Henry stared down at her hands, starting when the windshield wipers clicked on and thumped downward. The windshield was covered with a light mist, a typical Houston wet spell that couldn't rightfully be called rain.

The minivan pulled up to a red light. Gathering her courage, Henry turned. "About your—"

"About your—"

They laughed and Henry again noticed the corners of his eyes crinkled. The lines were endearing, proof he had a good sense of humor. He'd probably laughed a lot until his wife died.

"You first," she said quietly.

"No, you."

The light changed and the car eased into motion again. Henry pretended to study the windshield. "I'd like to hear about your wife. I usually appreciate the chance. People are always afraid to talk to me about my husband."

"I know what you mean. Once the funeral was over, hardly anyone ever spoke Nancy's name again."

Henry nodded. "It's especially hard for the kids."

Rick pulled the minivan into a parking space at the bookstore. He shut off the engine and gave her a curious stare. "How many children do you have?"

"Two. Brian's thirteen and Cindy's eight."

He shook his head. "I had no idea."

Before Henry could reply, Rick stepped out and reappeared on her side. He opened the door then frowned. "I hope you don't take this as an insult."

"Why would you think that?"

His gaze flickered over her suit as she stepped out. "You're the career type."

"I'm still a woman."

Rick's eyes twinkled. "I hadn't forgotten."

Henry's high heels clicked as she and Rick made their way across the wet asphalt and into the bookstore. Bright lights, classical music, and the aromatic fragrance of brewed coffee jolted her senses. Rick led the way to the café counter, and they paused to consider the list of exotic coffees and desserts.

"Hungry?" he said.

Henry made a face. "After cracking those eggs? No way!"

"Two hazelnut coffees, please," Rick said to the teenage girl behind the counter.

"Cream and sugar is at the next counter," the girl said indifferently, pouring coffee into thick mugs.

"Thanks." Rick counted out money then handed Henry her coffee.

She took a tentative sip of the steaming liquid. "Ummm."

Rick leaned against the counter, watching her. He smiled. "I'll bet you usually take cream."

Startled, she lowered her cup. "How'd you know?"

"All good executives do." He grinned. "At least the women. Men act like they have to prove something. They usually drink theirs black."

Henry ambled to the near counter. She used a light hand to pour cream, then held out the small pitcher. "And you? Do you have something to prove?" she teased.

"Me? No way." Still grinning, he took the pitcher and added a few drops to his cup. "I'm just an architect."

Henry took a long swallow to hide her pleasure. So he was artistic, after all. "What do you design?"

"Office buildings, mostly. My most recent work was the Stanhope Building."

"Really?" She looked at him with new respect. "I

read how it won several awards. It's right next door to my bank."

"Then you must work at First Houston."

"Personal trust. I handle estates." She sipped her coffee. "At least the business aspect wasn't a surprise when Les died."

Rick's eyes glowed with sympathy. "Your husband?"

Henry nodded, tightening her grip around the mug. "He's been dead a year, come January. The kids and I moved down here from Nebraska. My sister's my only living relative, and I wanted to be near family."

"It helps. Fortunately, my parents still live here. Still go to the same church, even. They help out, but you know how difficult it is with kids."

Henry set her mug down with a thump. "You have children?"

Rick's mouth curved upward. "Does that surprise you?"

"I didn't make the connection. The minivan was so clean, I thought it was used to carry architectural projects or something."

Rick laughed. "*Or something* is more like it. I have four children."

"*Four?*"

"Graham's fifteen, Rachel's fourteen, John's nine, and Clara's two."

"My, my," Henry lifted her cup and took a long swallow. And she thought she had it rough!

"They're good kids," Rick said. "Graham and Rachel especially pitched in to help out when Nancy died."

Henry softened. "What happened to her?"

Rick toyed with his plastic stirrer. "The doctors found the cancer when she was pregnant with Clara, but there wasn't much they could do. She went fast after the baby was born."

"I'm so sorry," Henry whispered, absentmindedly laying a hand over his. "It must have been very difficult."

Rick glanced down. Embarrassed, she drew her hand away, but he clasped it in his own. "What about your husband?" he said gently.

"Car accident. He was going to the store, and he got hit by a drunk driver. He died before they could get him to a hospital."

"At least I had some warning," Rick murmured.

"I don't suppose it makes the pain any easier to take. Sometimes I miss him so much, I think about going to the backyard to scream my head off."

"Me, too."

Henry drew a deep breath to steady herself. It'd been a long time since she'd fallen apart, and she wasn't about to do it here—in the middle of a bookstore—with a near stranger. But he seemed to understand her grief.

"The worst," she said tentatively, "is that I feel like it's my fault."

"How do you figure that?"

Henry studied their clasped hands. "Les was a home-based freelance writer. He loved the whole domestic bit. . .cooking, cleaning, PTA meetings, car pools. . . everything. So I worked at an office and he took care of the home front. But if I'd been the homebody, maybe that accident wouldn't have happened."

Henry felt the pressure of Rick's hand increase. "That's ridiculous. You were doing what you enjoy and so was he. Would you want him to feel guilty if you had been hit on a downtown street during your lunch break?"

"N-no."

Rick's hazel eyes shone warmly, gold flecks dancing. The crinkles had reappeared in a smile of sympathy.

"Finish your coffee," he said. "I'll be right back."

Henry obediently lifted her mug, swallowing the lukewarm liquid. Rick released her hand and headed for the book rows on the other side of the coffee area. She watched as his brown head disappeared among the stacks.

She swiveled her stool around to face the counter. What was wrong with her, anyway, to pour out her heart like that? She didn't have to make a fool of herself just because she and Rick had both lost a spouse, went to the same church, and couldn't cook!

Henry drained the mug and drifted outside the low iron rails separating the café from the bookstore. She glanced through several bargain coffee-table art books while keeping an eye out for Rick.

He soon reappeared, carrying a bag. To her surprise, he withdrew a hardback, placing it in her hands. "I want you to have this. It helped me a lot after Nancy died. I still read it occasionally when I feel down."

"*Blessed Are Those Who Mourn.* I've enjoyed several of this preacher's books already, but I've never heard of this one."

"I think you'll find it helpful. Read it, then get back

to me. We can talk some more."

She felt the warmth of gratitude. "Thank you. That's very thoughtful."

Rick smiled. "We'd better get back. Graham and Rachel may have lost their good humor about baby-sitting, and your kids probably want to see you some more tonight, too."

Henry laughed. "They like to see me, but not anywhere near the kitchen. I made a meat loaf tonight that may turn them both into vegetarians."

Rick's eyes warmed. "Then you'll just have to be sure to come back to cooking class next week, won't you?"

They rode back to the church in companionable silence. At the lot, Henry pointed out her car, and Rick pulled up alongside.

"Be careful on the way home. There are a lot of kooks in this city."

Henry's fingers gripped the spine of the book. "Thank you, Rick. For the coffee, the book, and most of all, the sympathetic ear."

"Any time," he said softly.

He stared at her a moment, and her heart lurched. Surely he wouldn't kiss her!

Her heart fell back in place. The thought was more appealing than she liked to admit.

Rick leaned back against his door and smiled. "Why do you call yourself Henry?"

She grinned, relieved the tension had broken. "My real name's Henrietta."

Without waiting for a reply, she opened the door.

four

Mary Alice peered at her sister through a singed, bottom-less copper teakettle. "Tell me again how this happened."

"I decided to use some of that potpourri you boil in water. You remember that autumn-scented stuff we both got at the mall?"

Mary Alice nodded. "Go on."

"Well, just before breakfast last Saturday I mixed some with water in the teakettle. Just like the directions said."

"Uh-huh."

"And I put it on the stove."

Mary Alice quirked a brow. "Did you set the burner on high?"

"Of course not! I put it on low."

"And then. . . ?"

Henry sighed. "And then later when I went to heat up some soup, I accidentally brushed my hand against the burner. Did I show you the blister I got on my finger? It popped just yesterday, but—"

"The teakettle?" Mary Alice prodded.

"Oh. Well, after I got through dancing around because of the blister and holding my finger under cold water, I remembered the kettle. I picked it up, but the bottom stuck to the burner. It could have happened to anybody!"

Mary Alice closed her eyes as though sending up a prayer for patience. "What time did you remember the kettle?"

Henry shrugged. "Dinner time."

Mary Alice groaned. "You left it on the stove all day?"

Henry grinned. "I guess so."

"You *guess* so?" Mary Alice waved the pot at her sister. "You could have started a fire!"

"But I didn't!"

"No, but you sure did over here." Mary Alice stepped from the kitchen to the fireplace in the living room. She tapped a foot next to a burned spot in the rug. "What happened here?"

"Oh, that." Henry waved her hand. "The kids and I were watching the football game Sunday, and I decided to build the first fire of the season. But apparently I put too much wood on the grate, because in minutes we had an absolute blaze."

"Did a spark jump out?"

"No. The fire was so big, I decided to take out one of the logs with the tongs."

Mary Alice covered her face. Her shoulders shook.

"It's not that funny!" Henry put her hands on her hips. "I tried to make it to the porch, but the burnt end of the log fell off. If Brian hadn't been there to stamp it out, the hole would have been even larger!"

Mary Alice lowered her hands. "You don't just need a man. You need a *fire*man!"

"Very funny," Henry mocked, her voice rising in exasperation. "And please stop laughing!"

"I'm sorry." Mary Alice wiped away a tear. "You did

ask me here to watch your kids, not to criticize."

"Yes," Henry softened, giving her sister a tentative smile. She grabbed her purse and headed toward the door. "I'll try not to be so late this time."

"Don't worry about that," Mary Alice called cheerfully. "If Rick asks you out for coffee again, by all means go."

Henry shut the door firmly and turned back to her sister. She narrowed her eyes. "What do you know about Rick?"

"I hear the talk. And you've obviously changed from your business suit to a very feminine dress. Come on, Henry, the least you could do is tell your own sister before I have to hear the gossip at church."

Henry groaned. "What gossip?"

"You two were seen heading out together for coffee after your first class last week. It seems you're cooking partners." Mary Alice grinned. "Or should I say you're *cooking?*"

Henry ignored her sister's teasing. "Who told you about the coffee?"

"April."

"April. . .April. . ." Henry failed to remember that name from her class. "April who?"

"April Logan. She heard it from Carole Swanson."

"Carole?" Again Henry drew a blank.

"She heard it from Mary Black. . ."

"I don't know any Mary!"

". . .who heard it from Vera Fabbish."

Henry groaned. "Not Vera!"

Mary Alice winked. "You'd better watch out. The

lady not only knows how to cook, she's the world's best manipulator. She'll have you and Rick married before you know it."

"That's ridiculous!"

"Vera grew up with his parents," Mary Alice said. "Apparently Rick's only recently started coming back to church."

Henry softened. "Because of his wife?"

Mary Alice nodded. "He and Pastor Reynolds talked for several months, and now Rick wants to be an active member again."

Henry shook her head. She didn't have any business listening to this! She crossed her arms. "Is nothing about the man safe from gossip?"

Mary Alice's lips twitched. "You'd better move fast. He's not seeing anybody. Yet."

Henry gasped in exasperation. "Oh, really?" She yanked open the door. "Well, tell Mary and Carole and April. . .and whoever else. . .not to hold their breath."

Mary Alice laughed. "Henry!"

"*What?*"

Her sister smiled. "I hope you're holding yours."

"Dreamer!" As if she had time for a man!

❧

Rick was already aproned and arranging cooking utensils when Henry sidled up to the counter.

"Sorry I'm late, partner." Henry drew on an apron, tying it behind her neck. "What's on the menu tonight?"

He smiled. "Pumpkin pie. Since Thanksgiving's next week, Vera liked the idea."

"Mmm. Pumpkin pie is my favorite part of the holiday."

She fumbled with the ties at her waist. "Wouldn't you know it? I think I've managed to knot this."

"Here. Let me."

Henry turned around and felt the warmth of Rick's hands on her back as his fingers worked nimbly at the knotted canvas. As he bent his head, she caught a whiff of cologne. She closed her eyes. A wave of nostalgia washed over her as she identified the scent. It wasn't what Les had usually worn, but it smelled clean and masculine.

He fastened a tight bow, and she turned back around. His gaze flickered over her apron and the soft blue dress underneath. "What happened to the suit?"

Henry glanced down, feeling like a high school girl. "I. . .uh. . .thought this might be more comfortable."

Rick's eyes warmed. "You look—"

Vera Fabbish appeared from nowhere and laid a hand on each of their shoulders. "How was the coffee?" she boomed.

All other conversation stopped and the rest of the class turned their way. Henry was certain her ears glowed red.

"The coffee was fine," Rick said casually.

"Good. Good. Now let's get to that pie." Vera winked at him then waddled to the head of the counter. "Attention, everybody. Let's begin. First, you take. . ."

Henry and Rick worked together, following Vera's instructions. Occupied with measuring, mixing, and stirring, they didn't have any further time to speak. They'd scarcely poured the batter into the pie shell and congratulated themselves on their success when Vera whisked the completed pie from their hands.

"We'll bake all of these overnight and use them in the church's soup kitchen tomorrow," she said, lining up the pies by the oven.

"Is that what happened to all those eggs we cracked?" someone called out.

Vera nodded. "They made great scrambled eggs the next morning."

"Probably not my eggs," Henry whispered. Rick laughed and Vera shot them an approving look.

"Even your eggs, Henry," she said warmly. "Except the one you gave to Rick as a manicure."

Everyone laughed, and flush with the apparent success of their pie, Henry laughed along with them. This cooking business wasn't so bad, after all. Now she could bake something that at least *looked* edible.

Vera waved her hands. "Class dismissed. See you next week."

Henry reached behind to untie her apron, but Rick was already loosening the bow. "Can I interest you in another discussion over coffee? Or do you need to get back to your kids?"

She turned. "I'd love some coffee. I finished that book you gave me."

"Great." He smiled. "That gives us a topic to start with."

The drive in the still-unwashed minivan was more animated than their first. They discussed not only the book, but a current spy movie, Pastor Reynolds' Sunday sermon, and the merits of business lunches at several downtown restaurants. Rick told her about his architectural work, and she proudly related her accomplishments at First Houston while they waited in line for their coffee.

"My job has been good therapy since Les died," she said. "And I'm working hard to get a vice presidency."

He handed over a full mug, and they settled at the counter. "Why?"

Henry thought for a moment. "Security."

"Financial, you mean?"

She nodded as she sipped. "It's not just the money, though. It's the position. With two kids to raise and put through college by myself, I have to make sure I'm indispensable. That way the bank can't ever fire me."

Rick stared at his mug as he swished the plastic stirrer in his coffee. "Don't you ever want to get more involved with your kids? Do PTA stuff?"

"I spend time with them. We play ball together, go to church. . .the same family bonding as everyone else. We just get together in the evening and on weekends like most single-parent families."

Rick still didn't look up. "If you didn't have to work, would you?"

"Yes." She laughed. "You already know I can't cook. I'm sorry to say the rest of my domestic capabilities are also sadly lacking. Even if I could manage, I don't think I'd be happy wrangling dust bunnies all day."

Rick didn't say anything.

When he dropped her off at her car, he still seemed quieter than when they'd first left. Henry took his silence for end-of-the-day weariness; she, however, was sorry to see the evening end.

"Thanks again for a wonderful time."

He smiled faintly. "Guess I'll see you next week. You did a good job on that pie tonight."

"*We* did a good job."

Rick cleared his throat and opened her car door. "Be careful driving home."

"I will."

He carefully shut the door. Smiling to herself, Henry started the engine. For the first time in a long while, she felt happy.

ಶ

The next few weeks passed slowly, even though work kept Henry busier than ever. She handled not only her own customers but several others from overburdened co-workers.

Yet every time the phone rang, she scrambled for the receiver, only to hear about another estate crisis.

Why didn't Rick call?

Sitting at her desk, she nibbled on the end of her pen. She'd certainly thought she and Rick had something going, but apparently he didn't think so. He was exceedingly polite and even joked with her while they stumbled through each class, but he never again offered to take her out.

She opened another folder with determination. So he wasn't interested. She'd never become a vice president by mooning over a man like a love-struck girl.

A knock sounded at her door. "Mrs. Steelman?" The door swung inward and Louise appeared with an apologetic look. "I'm sorry to interrupt, but there's a woman to see you who claims she's here about the Montgomery estate."

Henry leafed through the folders on her desk, bewildered. "I'm not handling any Montgomery estate."

"She's awfully insistent. If you don't mind my saying so, I think you should speak with her."

Henry glanced at the stack of folders and sighed. "All right. Send her in."

She quickly scanned her desk for neatness and then she rose. Before she could adjust her suit jacket, a large figure swathed in a bright blue Mexican housedress swept into the office and firmly closed the door in Louise's face.

"Vera Fabbish!"

"Sit down, dear." Vera motioned at Henry's chair then plopped herself in an opposite seat. "We've got some talking to do."

Perplexed, Henry sat. "What estate—"

"Rick Montgomery." Vera pulled her chair closer. "That man needs you."

Henry leaned back in shock, then straightened. "I hardly think that's any of your—"

"It's plenty of my business and then some!" Vera nodded for emphasis then pulled a handkerchief from her large vinyl purse to mop her neck. "Boy! It's really sticky outside. Even for December. Even for *Houston!*"

Henry gripped her pen for patience. "About Rick?"

Vera popped the handkerchief back in her purse. Leaning forward, she lowered her voice. "He's crazy about you."

"Crazy? About me?" Henry laughed. "We're not even what you could call friends! We're just in the same cooking class."

"Oh, you think that's all, do you?" Vera's mouth

curved in a superior smile. "Don't tell me you haven't noticed the way he looks at you. . .the way he makes excuses to get closer to you. Why, at the last class, even I could see from clear across the room how he held your hands."

"He was just showing me how to hold the cleaver." Henry hated to admit it, but she *had* felt a tingle.

"Then how do you explain the fact that he told his parents he met someone at his cooking class he wanted to date?" Vera smiled triumphantly as though she'd just baked a perfect soufflé.

Henry's heart lifted hesitantly. "He said that?"

Vera nodded with authority, blinking like an owl. "He said that."

Henry's heart crashed. "But we only went out twice for coffee. Surely he must have meant someone else."

"There isn't anyone else." Vera leaned forward. "But I have it on authority he won't ask you out because you're not domestic enough. He doesn't want to get serious about someone who isn't. He knows you can't cook. And he's heard rumors you can't keep house, either. Something about a copper kettle and a burned rug?"

Henry jammed the pen back into the holder. He'd avoided her because she didn't like keeping house? Because she wasn't Betty Crocker?

She struggled to keep her voice low. "I have a good job. I take good care of my kids. I *love* my kids. Isn't that what counts?"

"You don't have to tell me. You just have to convince Rick."

"*Convince* him?" Henry rose and flattened her palms on the desk. "I don't have to convince him of anything!

I'm not some helpless female from the nineteenth century who needs a man to take care of her! And I don't need his caveman attitude!"

Vera stood. "But, dear, I'm here to help you. I wanted to offer you cooking lessons on the side. Maybe some housekeeping tips, too."

"I like the man, but I'm not auditioning to be his maid. So you can tell his parents or April or. . . February. . .or whoever else is in your gossip group that I'm not interested!"

Vera sighed, clutching her bulky purse. "All right, dear. I was hoping it would work out, but apparently not. Don't let what I've said destroy your friendship, though. You two really do work well together. Out of all my students, you and Rick have shown the most improvement."

Henry's anger dissipated like steam from a hot pan plunged in ice water. "Really?"

"Really." Vera nodded. "Good-bye, dear." She shuffled out of the office.

Deflated, Henry slumped to her chair. Imagine all those people trying to throw her into Rick Montgomery's arms. And worrying that she didn't have the domestic skills he needed!

Henry straightened the items on her desk with unusual interest, swiping at a layer of dust. "It doesn't matter. If Mr. Montgomery is interested in love, he'd better call a housekeeping service!"

five

"I give up," Mary Alice said, laying down her fork. "What is it?"

Henry's face fell. "Tuna casserole."

"This is tuna?"

"Benjamin!" Mary Alice poked her husband in the side.

"I thought it was chicken!"

Brian giggled along with his cousins, Caroline, David, Robert, Stephen, and Alison. "You did it again, Mom," he said, brandishing a fork.

Cindy slid out of her chair and stood next to Henry. "I like it," she said solemnly. "Especially the potato chips."

"Thank you, Cindy." Henry gave her a quick hug.

"But Dad always crunched the chips in the tuna casserole, brainless." Brian made a face at his sister. "You're not supposed to just throw them on top!"

"You're the brainless one. Brainless Brian, brainless Brian!"

"That's enough!" Henry said. "And Brian, if you didn't like the casserole, why'd you have two helpings?"

Cindy snickered and returned to her chair. Henry flashed her a disapproving look, but she inwardly smiled at her daughter's defense. At least somebody appreciated her attempts.

Mary Alice sighed. "I wish we weren't going to Ohio

for Christmas. It doesn't seem right to leave you three alone."

"We'll manage," Henry said. "You need to be with your mother-in-law. After all, she's in a nursing home, and she especially needs family this time of year."

Mary Alice bit her lip. "Can't I at least fix you a dinner in advance? Something you could heat up for Christmas Eve and Christmas Day?"

"Nonsense! Vera showed us how to fix a turkey and green beans. We'll have a Christmas Eve feast that can't be beat!"

"Yeah. Literally."

"Brian!"

"Excuse me." He threw his napkin down and bolted from the table. He dashed down the hallway for his room. They heard the door slam, followed by a radio's blare.

Benjamin gave Henry a pointed look. "That boy needs disciplining. His attitude will just get worse as he gets older."

Henry collected plates with more force than necessary. "He's not a horse I'm trying to break. He's just a teenage boy trying to understand why his father had to die so suddenly."

"Of course he is," Mary Alice said soothingly, casting her husband a reproving glance. "But he is growing up, Henry. He hates it when you send me over here to baby-sit for him and Cindy. He's big enough to take care of them both. He is thirteen."

Henry stopped short. "I hadn't noticed how much he'd grown up. We've spent the past year just trying to cope with everything."

She set the plates down. "I need to talk to him right now."

Henry followed the radio's screeching electric guitar down the hall. As usual, Brian's door was closed. Hand poised to knock, she stared at the "No Trespassing" sign as if for the first time. Why had she let her son hide in there so long? She and Cindy were resilient enough to nurse their hurt alone and together, as needed. Somehow, she'd ignored Brian's veiled pain.

She knocked on the door, then pounded with her fist when she knew she hadn't been heard. "Brian? Open up. We need to talk."

"Go away!"

"Brian, please open the door. I don't care what you said about my cooking. I want to talk to you about something else."

The music abruptly clicked off and the door opened a crack. Eyes red, Brian stared at her through the sliver of space.

"Either let me in or you come out," she said quietly.

He stepped back, shrugging. "Whatever."

"Thanks." She stepped into his private lair. Dirty clothes littered the floor, and a half-eaten sandwich moldered on the cluttered dresser. Henry pushed down her dismay. A reprimand could come later.

She casually pushed aside several pairs of blue jeans and sat on the unmade bed. "It's been pretty difficult for you since Dad died, hasn't it?"

Brian scuffed the toe of his sneaker at a pile of dirty T-shirts. "I still miss him," he said grudgingly. He offered a bleak smile. "I'm sorry I've teased you about your cooking. I know you're doing the best you can. It's just. . ." He turned away. "It's just not the same. Nothing's the same."

"It'll never be like it was when your father was alive," Henry said. "Not just the cooking, but everything. If we all pitch in and do the best we can, I think one day we'll find ourselves happy again."

Brian turned back. "You're not happy? I know you miss Dad and all, but you're always so cheerful. And you never cry. I thought I was the only one who couldn't handle it."

Henry smiled. "I'm happy because I still have you and Cindy. And I cry, but not when you're around. I didn't want you to know I was still having trouble, too. Maybe that's our problem. . .not telling each other how we feel."

She cleared her throat. "Speaking of which, your aunt tells me you've been upset about her staying with you and Cindy when I go to cooking class."

Brian straightened. "I'm big enough to look out for us. We don't need Aunt Mary Alice to baby-sit!"

"No, I guess you don't." Henry stopped herself from ruffling his hair. "When my cooking classes resume after the holidays, we won't call her anymore."

"Can I get paid for watching Cindy?"

Henry grinned. "No. But I'll be glad to pay you for doing extra chores around the house, like painting or cleaning screens."

"Aww, Mom!"

Rising, Henry glanced around the room. When had the Donald Duck posters turned into movie heroes, the curtains from trains to a sedate solid color? She could remember Brian passing from elementary school to junior high, but when had he changed, too?

"This will be a rough Christmas," she said softly. "And I'm taking some extra time off around the holidays. The three of us can start new traditions this year."

"I'll still miss Dad." Brian sniffled once, then tentatively put his arms around his mother.

Henry kissed his wet cheek and held him close, grateful for the hug. "So will I, Brian," she murmured.

২৹

They missed him more than they could have possibly predicted. They missed not only his presence, his laughter, his singing Christmas carols off-key, but his ability to place the star on the top of the seven-foot-high tree.

Henry stretched on her toes but she lost her balance and fell into the tree, knocking it over. After disentangling herself from the sticky pine branches, she took one look at the puddle of spilled water and wanted to cry. Instead, she blithely asked Cindy and Brian to fetch towels while she placed the star on the tree—still laying on its side—then smugly righted it.

They missed Les when they took their annual drive to see the Christmas lights. He had known all the best neighborhoods and always took the family out for hot chocolate afterward. But Henry couldn't find any good light displays, and she forgot to bring her purse.

The worst disappointment of all occurred on Christmas Eve. Their tradition was to eat their big meal and open presents that night, then help in the soup kitchen on Christmas Day. Christmas Eve dinner was always ham, and Henry thought it fortuitous that Vera had taught the class how to cook a turkey. Maybe the change in menu would be good for the family.

Proud as a new mother, she lovingly basted the bird and shoved it into the oven before breakfast. By noon the turkey still looked raw.

"That's funny." Henry tested with her hand. "It still feels cold." She shrugged. "Oh well, back in the oven!"

Four hours later, the bird had scarcely pinkened in color. Henry's fears mounted, but she kept a cheerful front and turned up the oven's heat.

Two hours later, she was ready to cry. Instead of warm, juicy white meat, the bird could barely be stabbed with a knife.

Cindy tugged at her sleeve. "Mom? Maybe you were supposed to thaw the turkey first."

Henry exhaled with exasperation. "Of course! Any idiot would have known that."

Brian grinned. "What if we start a new tradition by having pizza on Christmas Eve?"

"That's hardly fitting for such a special holiday."

"Please, Mom?" Cindy's eyes shone. "That'd be fun. Like a special treat."

Henry softened at Cindy's pleading. "I guess we could always eat the green beans along with—the green beans!"

She dashed for the stove and flung the lid from the saucepan. Smoke hit her face. She coughed, waving her hand. Blackened mush stuck to the bottom of the pan.

Dismayed, Henry stepped back from the stove. What

kind of a mother was she, anyway, to burn half a holiday meal and undercook the other half?

She leaned against the counter, shoulders shaking as she suppressed her tears. *Oh, Les, how you'd laugh at me. You used to think it was cute that I couldn't cook, and you joked about being my protector in the kitchen. But it's not funny anymore.*

She felt a hand on her arm. "It's all right," Brian said. "You go get the pizza. Cindy and I'll clean up the kitchen."

"Can I have pepperoni?"

Henry glanced from Brian's face to Cindy's, both lit with hope and the wonder of the season. They obviously didn't care about the menu. Maybe she shouldn't, either.

"They say Christmas is a time to forgive." With a sigh, she reached for her purse.

෯

Henry clutched her red wool coat close as she scurried into the pizza parlor. She'd thought about ordering ahead or even having the pizza delivered, but decided in favor of the extra time alone. She'd nearly broken down in tears there in the kitchen. If she started crying, Cindy and Brian might, too. Then they'd all be miserable.

A bell tinkled as she pushed open the door. At least these people were happy. The jukebox blared "Jingle Bell Rock," and all the employees wore Santa stocking caps and had holly pinned to their uniforms.

"Merry Christmas!" A teenage boy grinned broadly. "What kind of pizza are you ordering to leave for Santa?"

Henry smiled in spite of her gloom. "He's told my

family he wants one pepperoni and one cheese. Both medium, thin crust."

"Coming right up. There's coffee by the jukebox while you wait."

Henry shivered, remembering the chill outside. "Thanks."

She wandered to the coffeemaker and poured herself a large Styrofoam cupful. She reached for the artificial creamer when a masculine hand covered hers.

"You mean you even drink this poor imitation of coffee?"

Heart thumping, Henry gazed up into a teasing face. "Rick! What are you doing here?"

He shrugged boyishly, handing over the creamer. "The same as you. Waiting for Christmas Eve dinner."

Henry glanced around the restaurant. "Is your family here?"

"No, I ordered carryout just a few minutes ago." He shoved his left hand into the pocket of his overcoat, and Henry noticed his right hand held a nearly full cup of coffee.

She nodded at an empty booth. "Why don't we wait together?"

He smiled in reply, following as she slid across a red vinyl cushion. He sat on the other side of the table, raising his eyes to meet hers.

"How've you been, Henry? I haven't seen you since our last class. I haven't even seen you at church on Sundays."

"I've been going to the early service." She sipped her coffee and shrugged. "And I've been all right."

Rick covered her free hand with his. "The first Christmas is rough."

She bowed her head. "Yes. It's been one disaster after another."

"Want to tell me about it? You're talking to someone who's been there." He paused. "Who's still there."

"It's still hard even after a couple of years, isn't it?"

"Yes." He glanced out the window. "I came here to get away from the kids for a few minutes. I needed some time alone to think about Nancy. Christmas was always special to her."

Henry smiled. "It was for Les, too. It's just not the same without him. Everything's different."

"Even the cooking?" Rick smiled faintly, teasing.

Henry returned the grin. "Especially the cooking. Why do you think I'm here?"

Rick laughed and squeezed her hand. "You're one of a kind, Henrietta Steelman."

Henry felt the warmth of his hand rush through her, a soothing balm to her wounded heart. "You're one of a kind, too, Rick," she said softly. "Not many men would take a cooking class so they could learn to feed their family better."

They fell silent. Rick clasped her hand in both of his. "Why've you been so quiet during the last few weeks of class? You don't strike me as the type to suddenly turn shy."

Henry's pulse raced. "I didn't want you to think. . ."

"What? That you were interested in me?"

Henry nodded. "Vera said you didn't want to date me because I wasn't domestic enough."

He looked at her a long moment. "Vera Fabbish is a busybody," he said in a low voice. "Will you go with me to the New Year's Eve party at church?"

She felt hypnotized. His hazel eyes made her feel like a schoolgirl all over again. He might as well have asked her to the junior prom.

"I'd love to go," she whispered.

"Montgomery! Your pizzas are ready!"

Rick smiled and released her hand. "I'll pick you up a week from tonight. Seven-thirty."

Henry nodded. They moved to the counter. Rick paid the boy, then reached for his pizzas.

Just before his hands gripped the cardboard, he turned. "Merry Christmas, Henrietta," he said softly, then leaned over and brushed his lips across her cheek.

Before she could react, he pointed at the ceiling above the cash register. Mistletoe hung from the ceiling.

Stunned, Henry tried to compose herself. "Merry Christmas to you, too."

She watched as he ferried the cartons to the door. The bell tinkled merrily as he exited, and she turned back to the cash register with a sigh.

"Your pizzas are ready, too," the boy said, plunking down two cartons. He glanced over her shoulder at the door and grinned. "Did Santa bring you a boyfriend?"

"I'm not sure," she said, still bewildered. "I'm beginning to hope so."

six

"You've got a date!" Dreamy-eyed, Cindy stared at Henry's reflection in the mirror.

"A minivan just pulled up in the driveway," Brian yelled from the front hallway.

"It's not really a date, Cindy," Henry said, rising from the vanity stool. She checked herself in the mirror a final time then reached for her evening bag. Funny. Her hands were trembling. "It's more like a. . .a. . ."

"He's getting out of his car!"

Henry took a deep breath and patted her hair. Cindy tugged at her hand. "Come on!"

"He's coming up the walk!"

Henry rounded the corner and saw Brian peering out the front door's peephole. Cindy bounced on the toes of her sneakers. "Mom's got a date! Mom's got a date!"

"Cindy," Henry said sharply. "It's not a—"

The doorbell rang.

Everyone froze. Brian pulled back from the door as if in shock, and Cindy's squeaky shoes silenced. Henry nervously smoothed the skirt of her crepe dress. "Open the door, Brian."

He threw her a tormented look then yanked open the door.

"Hi. You must be Brian."

"Yeah," he mumbled, stepping back. He shot Henry

48

a killing glance.

Henry stepped forward. "Come in, Rick." Her voice seemed an octave too high.

Rick entered, smiling. He held out a long-stemmed yellow rose. "A belated welcome to Texas."

She accepted the flower, inhaling its fragrance with appreciation. "How lovely. And especially this time of year. Thank you."

His dancing eyes met hers, and she inhaled sharply. Under his opened black coat he wore a stylish light charcoal suit. Freshly polished black shoes complemented the outfit. His gaze flickered over her as well, and she was glad she'd chosen the simple elegance of a basic black dress and pearls.

Rick cleared his throat, turning to Brian and Cindy. "Did you two have a good Christmas?"

Cindy nodded. "I got a new Barbie doll."

"My daughter, Rachel, has a whole collection she's outgrown. But I'm sure she'd love to have you come play with them at our house."

Henry warmed at Rick's overture. Not only was he kind, he was suggesting the two families should get together.

"This is Cindy," Henry said, stepping beside her daughter. "And this is Mr. Montgomery. He's in my cooking class."

Cindy beamed. "Hello, Mr. Montgomery."

"And Brian."

Brian stared down at his shoes.

"Hello, Brian." Rick held out his hand. Startled, Brian glanced up. He gulped, then extended his own hand.

Cindy jammed her hands against her hips. "What about me? Mom says even women should learn how to shake hands. It's good business."

"Oh, is it?" Rick cocked an eyebrow at Henry, who hid a smile behind her rose. Rick made a serious face and extended his hand to Cindy. "How do you do, Miss Steelman? It's a pleasure to make your acquaintance."

"I'm very well." Cindy pumped his hand once and simultaneously nodded. "Thank you."

Smothering a laugh, Henry retrieved her coat from the closet. "Mr. Montgomery and I have to leave now. There are snacks on the counter and the number of the church is by the phone. You and Brian may stay up until midnight, then off to bed."

Brian straightened. "I'll take good care of Cindy. We'll watch the video you let us rent."

Rick took Henry's coat from her hands and held it up behind her. "Allow me."

She eased her arms into the sleeves and shrugged into the coat. He straightened the narrow collar, then his hands drifted downward to linger on her shoulders.

"Thanks," she murmured. The pressure from his hands unsettled her composure. He didn't seem in any big hurry to release her. She could almost feel him lean against her, could feel his lips near her hair.

Henry turned. Rick gazed down at her with a slow-spreading smile.

"Are you ready?" he said, taking her hand.

She nodded. "Have a good time, kids."

Rick turned to Brian and said soberly, "I'll take good care of your mom."

Brian nodded, straightening even more at the man-to-man assurance.

Rick kept a hand at Henry's elbow as they crossed the flagstone path to the driveway. When they reached the van, she burst out laughing.

He frowned. "What's wrong?"

Henry pointed, even though she knew it wasn't mature. "Your van. It's washed!"

"My father gave me a book of car wash coupons for Christmas."

Henry laughed. "I'll miss the heart on the door."

"That was Rachel's handiwork. She was mooning over some boy at school." He grinned. "You didn't think I drew it, did you?"

Flashing him a teasing glance, she shrugged. "How do I know what new architectural design you might be considering?"

Laughing, Rick shut the car door after her.

❧

Warm yellow lights bathed the outside of the fellowship hall. Henry was pleased the parking lot was full. All the adult Sunday school and community classes had been invited, and judging from the loud party chatter, many people had chosen to share the festive occasion. In just a few short hours, it would be a new year, with new possibilities and hope.

She smiled and Rick squeezed her hand. "Happy?"

She nodded. "It's been a long time since I've been to a party."

He studied her a moment. "Me, too," he said softly. "Too long."

They stepped up to the welcome table where a teenage girl took their coats for safekeeping. They had barely set foot inside the hall's doorway when Vera Fabbish broke away from a small knot of conversationalists.

"Well, look who's here!" her voice trumpeted as she advanced on them. She wore a tight black dress studded with iridescent sequins. A large, live poinsettia bloom perched behind her ear as though it had taken root at the back of her neck.

"Hello, Vera." Rick bent over and kissed her powdery cheek. As he straightened, she giggled, flushing, and turned to Henry.

"Isn't he a wonderful man? His parents are over there, dear. I know they'll be glad to meet you."

Oh, no. Henry had known people would whisper about her and Rick, but she hadn't realized his parents would be present.

Rick leaned closer. "Don't worry," he whispered, taking her hand again. He flashed a dazzling smile at Mrs. Fabbish. "Are you here alone?"

She fanned a ring-studded hand and giggled again. "Good gracious, boy. I'm here with *all* my friends!"

Rick laid a hand over his heart and rolled his eyes heavenward. "Surely there must be someone special? Mr. Graves the janitor, perhaps?"

To Henry's amazement, Vera flushed crimson. Her mouth opened and closed like a catfish, but no sound came out.

"Don't worry." Rick smiled, then leaned forward. "I won't tell," he whispered dramatically.

Vera's complexion returned to its natural color, and she drew herself to her full five-foot, four-inch height. "Richard James Montgomery, you'd better *not* breathe a word to anyone or I'll. . .I'll. . .tell your mother! Mr. Graves just doesn't know yet that I. . .I. . ."

"Adore him?" Henry put in, linking her arm through Vera's. "How will he know unless you tell him?"

"Well, I. . ."

"Of course," Rick put in, flanking Vera on the other side, "I suppose two well-meaning friends could speak on your behalf if you're shy."

Vera glared. "Don't you *dare!*"

Afraid any laughter would be construed as an insult, Henry pulled away. "We're only teasing, Vera. Please forgive us."

"We just want to see you happy," Rick added.

Vera glanced from him to Henry. "Seems to me I see two people who are awfully pleased with themselves," she grumbled. "Picking on a poor, defenseless old woman!"

Henry laughed gently. "Vera Fabbish, the day you're old and defenseless is the day I'll become a. . .a. . ."

"Cordon bleu chef?" Vera suggested mildly.

Henry laughed again. "Exactly!"

Rick took her arm to guide her away. "Have a good evening, Vera," he called over his shoulder.

Still chuckling, he led Henry to the punch bowl, where they accepted two full glasses from the server. Henry sipped from hers, noticing the crinkles hadn't faded from around Rick's eyes.

"You *are* awfully pleased with yourself, aren't you?"

she teased. "How'd you know about Mr. Graves?"

Rick laughed. "My mother told me. I really do want to see Vera happy. The woman's had a sad life. She never married and had kids of her own, so she tends to take people under her wing. Whether they want it or not."

"She's certainly taken a personal interest in us. She came all the way to my office to offer me extra cooking lessons and housekeeping tips."

"To snare me?" Rick asked, grinning.

"Something like that." Henry dropped her gaze to her punch.

She glanced at the few people clustered around the punch table, then backed away to the wall. Rick followed, smiling quizzically. "What?"

Henry set her glass on the windowsill. "We might as well set things straight right now. I'm sure that what Vera said was true. You're probably more interested in dating a domestic woman. Not someone who's all thumbs. . .and brown thumbs, at that."

Rick set his glass beside hers. He stretched out his hand as though to touch her, then glanced around and dropped it at his side. "Look, Henry," he said quietly. "You've jumped ahead of me, but you might as well know my intentions. I had some time to think these last few weeks. I do want to date you. I want to get to know you better. You may not be Betty Crocker, but you have a lovely woman's heart. You care about your kids, your job, and other people. Most of all, you laugh at yourself when you make mistakes and you keep trying. That's a very rare gift. Especially for someone in the business world."

His hazel eyes locked with hers as he moved closer, and she felt rooted to the floor. The room's conversations eddied around her, dropping to an indistinguishable hum.

"Since we're *setting things straight,* I'm going to give you fair warning," he continued, his voice low and husky. "I intend to kiss you at the stroke of midnight, Henrietta Steelman, from the first chime to the last. And I *will* see you again. . .as often as you'll let me. . . during the coming year. If you have any objections, say so now."

Henry's mouth went dry and her palms damp. What was wrong with her composure tonight? She was a career woman!

"Henry?"

She forced herself to breathe. "I want to see you, too, Rick," she whispered.

He held out his hand, smiling. "Good. Now that everything's straight between us, are you ready to mingle?"

Henry smiled and placed her hand in his. "Lead on."

And he did. Straight to his parents. Henry's stomach had barely righted itself when he led her across the room to a well-dressed older couple. She knew immediately from the family resemblance they were was Mr. and Mrs. Montgomery.

"Richard!" The man clapped a hand on Rick's shoulder. "So you made it, after all!" He smiled warmly at Henry, glancing from her then back to his son.

"I told you I was coming. And that you'd get a chance to meet—"

"How do you do, my dear?" The silver-haired woman interrupted, taking Henry's hand. "If we depend on these two, we'll never get acquainted. I'm Mary Montgomery."

"It's a pleasure to meet you, Mrs. Montgomery." Henry smiled at the woman's warmth. "I'm Henrietta Steelman."

The woman squeezed Henry's hand once more before releasing it. "Please call me Mary."

"Only if you'll call me Henry. Henrietta was my great-aunt's name."

"Henry?" Mr. Montgomery chuckled. "That was the name of my first business partner. It's a good, strong business name."

"Henry's a good businesswoman, Dad." Rick turned to her, smiling. "This is my father, Allen Montgomery."

Allen chuckled, pumping her hand several times. "The pleasure's all mine. Rick's been moping around the house for weeks now. Even the children have started to complain."

Mary smiled. "Have you met Rick's children, Henry?"

"No. We haven't known each other long."

Mary drew Henry aside, turning away from Rick and his father. The men started a spirited business discussion.

"Rick's been moping because of you, dear," Mary said softly. "He finally confessed when I pried it out of him." She paused, her eyes warm. "I hope you don't think I'm interfering by telling you. It's just that Rick's been so unhappy since Nancy passed away. When he first mentioned you, his face lit up like it hasn't for a long time. You're the first woman he's been interested in since she died."

"I feel the same way, Mary."

Rick wrapped an arm around each woman. "Hey, you two, no secrets!"

Mary playfully swatted her son on the shoulder. "No secrets, indeed. This is New Year's Eve. You two go chat with somebody closer to your own age. Have a good time. You don't want to stick around the old fogies."

Allen winked at Henry. "Besides, I think I saw Vera Fabbish coming this way. She claims she threw you two together. If you don't hurry, she'll start crowing and won't leave you alone all night."

"We already ran into her," Henry said.

Rick smiled. "She'll probably steer clear of us for a while."

Mary's face fell. "You didn't tease her about Mr. Graves, did you? Oh, Rick!"

"We only offered to help her budding romance by letting the poor man know her feelings. After all, she's meddled in our relationship already. Maybe it's time we helped her out."

"Don't you dare!" Mary took another swat at Rick, this time less playful. "Vera Fabbish is one of my oldest, dearest friends. If you upset her, you'll have to answer to me!"

Rick laughed and held up both hands. "All right, Mother. We promise to be good, don't we, Henry?"

"Yes, ma'am," Henry said solemnly, nodding.

Rick moved closer and casually draped an arm around her shoulder. "But we'll take your advice and make the rounds. See you two later."

"Good-bye, dear." Mary smiled at Henry. "It was

lovely meeting you. Don't wait for an invitation. Come over to the house any time."

"Thank you, Mary," Henry said. "It was nice meeting you, too, Mr. Montgomery."

"Allen. And the invitation goes double with me."

Henry and Rick chatted with fellow cooking students and their respective Sunday school class members, even making new friends. Though the church had three services every Sunday morning, people welcomed strangers like lifelong friends. Henry wondered how long it would have taken her to meet Rick if they had never signed up for the cooking class.

Several times during the night she surreptitiously glanced at her wristwatch. Her stomach danced every time she remembered Rick's promises for midnight. Would he really kiss her in front of all these people? How tongues would wag!

By eleven-thirty Henry and Rick sat at a large table. They had managed to avoid Vera all night, but she must have forgiven them. With a big smile, she plopped down in the chair next to Henry.

She glanced at Henry then Rick, who was involved in a discussion with the man seated next to him. She peered at Henry's watch and grinned. "You know what happens at midnight, don't you?"

Henry nearly choked on her punch. "Wh-what?" How could she have overheard their conversation?

Vera drew back in apparent surprise. "Why, we sing 'Auld Lang Syne,' that's what!"

"Oh, that!"

Vera eyed her suspiciously. "What did you think I meant?"

"I wasn't sure." Henry shrugged innocently. "I thought maybe the church had some special tradition."

Rick leaned forward. "What's this about tradition?"

"Vera and I were discussing midnight traditions. Do you know any?"

Rick winked at her.

Eleven-fifty. Someone brought out party hats and blowers. Eleven fifty-five. One of the servers filled all the glasses with punch for toasting. Eleven fifty-eight. Everyone pushed back from the table.

Rick lazily took Henry's hand and eased her away. "Come on, Henry. Let's—"

"Where do you two think you're going?" Vera clamped a hand on their arms. "You'll miss the party!"

Henry's stomach dropped. "But, Vera, we—"

"Nonsense!" She steered them back to the table. "I wouldn't dream of letting you miss the fun."

Miserable, Henry forced a smile.

"Everybody lift your glass," Vera commanded, raising hers.

Rick raised his glass and smiled apologetically at Henry. Disappointment knifed through her, not only from the lack of the kiss but from the expression on his face. He might kiss her good night at her door later, but it wouldn't be the same as at midnight.

"Oops!" She wobbled on a high heel and bumped into Rick. Punch splashed his shirt, and her eyes widened. "Oh, Rick, I'm so sorry!"

He dabbed at the spot with a napkin. "It's all right. It's—"

"Come on!" She grabbed his hand. "Excuse us, everybody! If we don't get the punch out right now, it'll make a permanent stain."

"But you'll miss the midnight celebration!" Vera wailed.

"Can't wait, Vera." Henry tugged at Rick's hand. "Let's go!"

They escaped through the maze of people, who ignored their departure in favor of the countdown. "Ten. Nine. . ."

Heels clicking against the linoleum, Henry pulled Rick down several well-lit halls to the darkened kitchen.

"Slow down!" Rick said. "It's just a little punch!"

She pulled him into the kitchen. Dim light spilled in from the hall and across the steel counters. Henry's heart pounded as she pulled him to the back of the room.

Even in the shadows she could see his face switch from confusion to understanding. He laughed. "You deliberately spilled that punch."

"You weren't going to kiss me in front of that mob, were you?"

Rick's laughter died out. He moved closer, his voice lowering. "It crossed my mind, but no, probably not. Especially with Vera watching us like a hawk."

They heard muffled shouts and blowers.

Rick pulled her close, then cradled her face in his hands. "You're a special woman, Henry," he murmured as his face moved closer. "Happy New Year."

"Yes. . .Happy New Year," she echoed just before his lips pressed against hers.

The pounding in her ears drowned out the faint strains of "Auld Lang Syne." She was certain her heart beat in sync with each stroke of midnight. But just when she thought the minute was up, Rick pulled back, only to kiss her again.

At last he broke the kiss, but he dropped his arms around her to pull her even closer. She encircled his waist with her arms. How different it felt to be with another man than Les, yet how right. Rick had revived the heart she'd thought had stopped for good, the heart she'd thought could never love again.

"Would it frighten you if I said I'm falling for you in a big way?" he said softly.

Henry pressed her cheek against his shoulder, reveling in the scratch of his wool jacket. What a safe, masculine touch.

"I'd only be frightened if you don't want to hear the same from me," she murmured. "I never thought I'd be so happy again."

"I didn't, either." His hand stroked her hair, and he nuzzled his cheek against her forehead. "This is why I wanted to kiss you at midnight. I want to begin the new year with you. I have a feeling this is going to be a great year."

"A *great* year," she echoed, raising her face for another kiss.

The kids were healthy, the bills paid, and now she had Rick. She'd work harder to get that vice presidency, then life would be complete.

seven

"And Mrs. Redwine called, and Mr. Tate, and. . ."

Henry absentmindedly accepted the pink telephone message slips from Louise, only half-listening to the secretary. She'd been back at work two weeks since the holidays, since New Year's Eve, and her heart still soared whenever she thought about Rick—which seemed to be all the time, lately.

"Then there's the Sampson estate." Louise plopped down a huge manila folder on the desk, jarring Henry back to reality. "You have a lunch date with Mrs. Sampson."

Henry blinked. She and Rick had planned to eat together. "Lunch? With Mrs. Sampson?"

Louise nodded, her blond curls swaying. She sat down tentatively, glanced over her shoulder, then quietly shut the door.

"Is everything all right, Mrs. Steelman? I know it's none of my business, but you've been in a fog since New Year's."

Henry grinned, leaning back. Ordinarily she sat ramrod straight in her high-back executive chair. But now she slumped casually, tempted to cross her ankles on top of her desk. She giggled at the thought and covered her mouth with steepled fingers.

Louise stared. "Mrs. Steelman?"

Henry picked her feet up and spun around in the

chair. "Whee!" She giggled again, then burst into out-right laughter at Louise's stunned expression. "I've always wanted to do that."

"Mrs. Steelman, are you *sure* you're all right?"

Henry steadied herself with a hand on the edge of her desk. "I'm fine," she said, smothering a final chuckle. "I'm. . ." She giggled again, covering her mouth. "No, I'm not fine. My stomach's in knots. How can I sit here and read through a stuffy file or concentrate long enough to have a business lunch?"

Louise gave Henry a sideways glance, a smile curving her lips. "It's that man you've been seeing, isn't it?"

Henry's face fell, all humor gone. "How'd you know?"

Louise shot her a smug look. "I'm a secretary, remember?" She grinned and shoved another stack of pink squares across the desk. "I especially notice when the man in question. . .Mr. Montgomery. . .provides me my job security. It's a good thing the voice mail is broken."

Henry picked up the slips and fanned them out on the desk. "He called this many times?"

Louise nodded. "And that's just from this morning when you were in the meeting with Mr. Fitzhugh! Each time he left a one-word message."

Henry fingered the four slips. The message from nine-ten said merely "Steelman;" nine-thirty, "mine;" nine-forty, "Henrietta;" ten o'clock, "be." Henry put the slips in logical order. "Be mine, Henrietta Steelman," she whispered.

Louise grinned. "The second time he called, he apologized for taking up my time."

"Be mine?" Henrietta whispered again. "What does that mean?"

Louise rose. "Sounds pretty serious." She paused. "Do you want me to come up with an excuse to cancel your lunch date?"

The door burst open, and Mr. Fitzhugh angrily stepped inside. He glared from Louise to Henry. "What's this about canceling lunch with Mrs. Sampson?"

Henry put on her business face. "Nothing, Mr. Fitzhugh. I just told Louise I had a bit of an upset stomach, and she wondered if maybe I should skip lunch and go home."

"Well?" Mr. Fitzhugh thundered.

Henry rose, resting her fingertips on her desk for support. "I'm fine, Mr. Fitzhugh. There won't be any problem with my lunch plans."

"Good! The Sampson estate is one of our most important. I would hate to have to give it to someone else because of your *stomach* problems."

He gave her one final glare then turned on the cowering Louise. "In the meantime, let the executives decide the fate of their own day, Mrs. Johnson."

"Y-yes sir," she whispered, eyes filling with tears.

Mr. Fitzhugh harrumphed one more time, then stomped out of the office. Louise leaned against the door, pressing her knuckles against her mouth. Henry moved swiftly from behind her desk to the secretary's side and laid an arm across her shoulder.

"Don't worry, Louise," Henry soothed. "He's just blowing steam."

Louise sniffled. "I'm sorry, Mrs. Steelman. I didn't mean to get you in trouble. I just thought you might want to have lunch with Mr. Montgomery instead."

Henry handed Louise a tissue. "He'll understand. I forgot all about this lunch date, that's all."

Louise blew her nose then drew a deep breath to regain her composure. "Thank you for covering for me. Mr. Fitzhugh probably would have fired me if you hadn't helped me out."

Henry grinned. "He'd probably have fired me, too. I don't think the man allows his employees to have a personal life."

❧

"Richard Montgomery," the deep voice said.

Henry smiled into the receiver. "Is this the Richard Montgomery who leaves women cryptic messages?"

Rick laughed. "Just certain women. Is this one of them?"

"Are you auditioning for a harem? When you said, 'Be mine,' I didn't realize it meant being one of a collection."

"It doesn't. To the best of my recollection, I haven't asked a girl to be mine since I had a crush on Suzie Knox in fourth grade."

Henry laughed. "And did Suzie accept?"

"Nope," he said cheerfully. "Turned me down flat for Pete Reston."

Henry's smile slipped. "What did you really mean by that message?"

She heard a chair squeak over the phone, indicating Rick had leaned back. "Why, I want you to be my girl," he said softly, his voice still retaining the hint of a tease.

"And what does that mean?"

"What do you want it to mean?"

"I'm not sure."

"Henry, you know I'm crazy about you," he said softly. "So crazy, all I can do is think about you. About your soft brown hair, your expressive gray eyes, the way your laugh turns husky when you're really happy, the way you walk in those skinny little heels. . . What more can I say?"

Henry swallowed hard. "Say you'll pick me up tonight for the cooking class."

"And dinner afterwards?"

Henry shook her head, then realized he couldn't see her over the phone. "I can't. It's a school night."

"Say you'll have dinner with me this weekend, then. At my place. You can meet my children."

Henry smiled. "Are you doing the cooking?"

"Yes, ma'am. Barbecue," he said proudly. "I operate a mean outdoor grill. It's the inside stuff I can't handle."

"It's a date then."

"Good. What time should I pick you up for lunch?"

Henry shifted uncomfortably. "I can't make it today. I forgot I have a business lunch."

"Oh." He put a lot of disappointment in that one-syllable word.

"Maybe tomorrow?" she said hopefully.

"The rest of the week is out. I have to go west of town every day to a construction site. I don't like to design from my office and never get a feel for the whole project."

Henry felt a rush of admiration. That was one of the things she admired about Rick. Part of the reason for his hard-earned respect in the architecture world was his refusal to sit in an ivory tower.

"I'll pick you up tonight," he said. "We might as well set Vera's tongue to wagging by showing up together for the first class of the new year."

"We do owe her the pleasure," Henry agreed, "after the way we teased her at the party."

The chair squeaked again over the phone. "Seven o'clock, then, Henry," he said softly. "I'll count the hours."

❧

That evening, Henry scurried around the house to get ready. She hadn't been able to leave the office at five o'clock, and the laundry was behind schedule. A clean, unfolded pile collected wrinkles on her bed, the drier hummed with another load, and water rushed in the washer over yet another.

Brian had to be nagged to clean up his room, Cindy spilled an entire glass of milk at dinner, and dirty dishes piled up in the sink like a stoneware Tower of Babel.

"Brian, rinse off the dishes then make the lunches for tomorrow. Cindy, you're big enough to run the vacuum cleaner. Clean up the living room and the den. I'll get the bedrooms and hallways later."

"But Mom, I have a science project due tomorrow!"

"And I have Girl Scouts tonight! Don't you remember? Betsy's mom is picking me up."

Henry held a hand against her throbbing head. "We have to get organized around here! We can't take care of this house, eat, and have time for all our activities when I don't come home until six-thirty."

Brian shrugged. "Why don't we get a maid? At least then we wouldn't have to worry about cleaning the house."

Henry stopped in her tracks. "You know how I feel about that. It's. . .it's *lazy* to have a maid, that's what it is!"

Brian shrugged again. "Maybe so, Mom, but it sure would help."

Staring at the pile of clothes on her bed, Henry sighed. Somewhere in there was the red sweater she wanted to wear tonight. Rick said he liked the way the color blended with her hair, and he hadn't seen the sweater yet. She lifted a wrinkled blouse. There didn't seem to be much point in digging through the pile; the clothes had sat neglected in the dryer for two days.

She sifted through the few occupied hangers in her closet. Too summery, too heavy for the warm day, too bright, too dark. . . Nothing seemed right for this evening.

Henry slumped on the bed beside the pile. "I give up. We'll just have to get a maid until things settle down."

"Hooray!" Brian called from the hallway.

"Neat," Cindy said, grinning. "I thought only rich people had maids."

"We're hardly rich." Henry shifted a few wrinkled clothes through her hands and sighed. "Just desperate."

略

"You're going to hire a maid?" Rick's voice was incredulous.

"It makes a lot of sense. I can afford it and it will help out around the house. Then I'll just have to worry about cooking and making sure everybody's where they're supposed to be at the right time."

Rick's jaw tightened in the glare of oncoming traffic. "Nancy never once asked for a maid, and she was busy with four kids and more volunteer work than she had a right to be."

Henry bristled, then relented. She'd been tempted to compare Rick with Les, too. "I'm not Nancy."

Rick sighed, groping for her hand while he kept an eye on traffic. "I'm sorry. You're right."

As they entered the church, they saw a large cardboard sign announcing the formation of the Bread and Fish program. Henry had volunteered to help get it started, but so far no one had contacted her.

"Looks like the soup kitchen's going to get a little competition," Rick said.

"It isn't supposed to compete. It's designed to reach out to the community." Henry said. "Rather than others coming to us, we're going to help people where they live. The homebound as well as the homeless."

Rick smiled and opened the door for her. "Sounds like a good idea. I'd like to help."

When they walked into the kitchen, the room burst into applause. Henry shrank back against Rick in surprise. Clapping the hardest was Vera Fabbish, who stepped out from the group with a wide grin on her face.

"Our class romance," she said proudly, bobbing her head at Henry and Rick. Henry smothered a giggle; Vera's hair was trapped in a sparkly silver cafeteria server's net, which contrasted with her pseudo-gold lamé dress.

"Hooray for Rick and Henry!" someone yelled.

"Calm down," Rick said, grinning. He casually put an arm around Henry and someone else whistled.

"We're just happy for you, dears," Vera said, drawing them to their appointed spot at the counter. "Prudence Standish told me how she caught you two coming out of the kitchen together after midnight on New Year's Eve."

She narrowed her eyes. "I wondered why you two were in such a hurry to get away when we toasted in the new year. I should have known it wouldn't be like Henry to worry about a little stain."

Rick sensed Henry's embarrassment and came to her rescue by lifting a green bean from the pile in front of them. "What are we learning to cook tonight? Or are we going to eat these raw?"

Schoolteacher serious, Vera took her place of authority at the head of the counter. "You learned how to cook green beans before Thanksgiving. Tonight we're going to take it a step further and make everyone's favorite green bean and mushroom casserole."

A few groans sounded around the room. "My mother bakes that for every holiday!"

Vera flashed a smug smile. "There's a reason for that, dear. It's not only easy to make, but *most* people like it. Now, we start by snapping the beans. . ."

❧

Brian dropped the clean laundry on the couch. He sighed in disgust as he plopped down on the opposite end then flipped on the television with the remote control. Stuporous, he sat in the darkness without turning on the lamp.

Cindy came through the front door, waving at the station wagon pulling away from the curb. "See you later!" The driver honked in reply and Cindy closed the door. She frowned at Brian in the darkened room.

"How was your old Girl Sprouts meeting?" Brian never took his eyes off the blaring set.

Cindy hugged her handbook with both arms. "We're going to go camping soon. At least. . . ," she paused. "I guess most of the girls will."

Distracted by a commercial, Brian glanced up to see his sister's tears. "What's the matter, Cinder-face?" he said gruffly.

Cindy sniffled. "It's supposed to be a father/daughter camp out. I guess I can't go."

Brian made a face. "Maybe what's-his-name will take you."

"Mr. Montgomery? Why would he do that?"

"Are you brain dead?" Brian snorted. "He's probably going to marry Mom."

Cindy's face turned white. "You mean he'd be our dad?"

"That's usually how it works." Brian turned back to the television and flipped channels aimlessly, shrugging. "I guess it could be worse."

"But I don't want another dad!" Cindy dropped the book to the floor and burst out in tears. "I want Daddy back!"

Brian gulped, then jabbed the channel button of the remote control. As he rapidly switched channels, he gradually increased the volume. The television's blare alternated feverishly between rock music, a sales pitch, and suggestive dialogue, gray-white light flashing in syncopation against the darkened room.

The harder Cindy sobbed, the faster the channels changed. The volume increased to ear-splitting level. Cindy screamed and covered her ears. Brian threw the remote control to the carpet, and the TV mercifully shut off.

Brian jerked to his feet and balled his fists at his sides. He glared at his wailing sister. "Grow up, Cindy!" he yelled, then stomped to his room.

eight

Henry smiled uneasily through the screen door at the teenage boy standing on the other side. He balanced a toddler on his hip, ignoring the little girl's tugs at his hair.

With effort, Henry increased the smile on her face. "Hi! You must be, um. . ." She cast about in her memory. "Graham?" She smiled at the girl. "And Clara?"

The boy continued to stare. The girl continued to ignore Henry, laughing as she tugged at her brother's curly brown hair.

Anxious, Henry tried to peer over the boy's shoulder without being obvious. Why didn't he invite her in? Did he think she was a salesperson?

"I'm Henry Steelman," she tried again. "Your father's expecting me. He invited me for dinner."

The boy flipped his hair back with a toss of his head and shifted the toddler higher. "Oh, yeah," he said flatly, pushing the screen door open with the toe of his sneaker.

"Thanks." Henry stretched her smile to its limits.

Boy and toddler faded down the hall without a backward glance. The door nearly slammed in Henry's face, but she squeezed through at the last moment, the side banging her blue jeaned hip.

"Great," she muttered under her breath, rubbing the

tender spot. "I'll probably have a bruise by tomorrow."

The words echoed in the empty hall. Henry glanced up and her eyes widened. Judging by the entryway alone, Rick's dwelling could appear in the pages of an interior decorating magazine.

Italian marble gleamed underfoot, flanked by muted green walls with white trim. On closer inspection, Henry discovered that the hall's only framed print was a limited edition—the first of one hundred—signed by a famous modern artist. She wished she'd paid more attention when her art appreciation class had studied his work.

"Wow," she murmured, turning slowly. What had Rick thought about the humble art book prints hanging in her own front hall?

"Henry? I didn't hear you come in."

She whirled around, her heart jumping.

Rick stood at the end of the hall, clad in typical weekend griller attire: a tall white chef's hat and a chest-to-knees canvas apron. He held a messy two-pronged fork in his hand. One look at his getup and Henry's heart dropped back in place. She burst out laughing.

"I happen to cook better in this outfit, thank you," he said haughtily. He bent over and whispered in her ear, "You have to do it, you know."

Bewildered, she drew a blank. "Do what?"

Rick pointed proudly at the words on his apron front. "Why, kiss the chef, of course."

Henry laughed and stepped closer. Rick's face sobered under the tall hat, and he wrapped an arm around her.

"Come here, you. I've been waiting for you all week."

"Mmm," she whispered in reply, drawing her arms around his neck. "Me, too. I've been—"

Her words died in her throat as his lips met hers, and his free hand pressed against the middle of her back.

Warmth rose inside her, the warmth of love and hope. And with it, an unfulfilled dream to not only capture a love as fine as the one she'd lost but to surpass it.

With this man. This incredibly handsome, brilliant, artistic man.

Who even now was dripping barbecue sauce down her back.

"Uh, Rick," she murmured, placing her hands on his chest.

"Mmm?" He bent for another kiss, pulling her closer.

She squirmed in his embrace, then seeing that she wasn't gaining his attention, placed her lips next to his ear. "The fork," she whispered in her best seductive voice. "It's dripping sauce on me."

His eyes flew open, and he jerked away to arm's length. "Oh, Henry, I'm sorry!" He turned her around. "Great. All down your back. And this is a silk blouse, isn't it?"

Henry tried to suppress a smile. "It *was* a silk blouse."

"I'm so sorry!" He brushed at the glob but only succeeded in spreading the stain.

"For once you made the mess." She laughed. "Don't worry about it, Rick."

"Send me the cleaning bill." He clucked his tongue. "Such a waste. It's a beautiful shade of red. And that print. I'll bet you can't find another one like it."

Henry smiled to herself. Men. What did they know about mail-order catalogues? She waved her hand. "Forget it. But maybe we'd better see if we can put some water on this thing to take care of the major damage."

"Better yet, I'll get you another shirt. Rachel's would be too small, but you can wear one of my sweatshirts."

Henry's humor instantly faded. "I wanted to look nice to meet your family."

He smiled warmly. "They're going to love you." He paused. "Just like I do."

Shocked, Henry forgot about her attire. "You love me?"

Rick nodded. "I think ever since you held out your hand and introduced yourself as Henry Steelman at that first cooking class." His expression sobered. "But maybe I shouldn't have said anything."

She wrapped her arms around him. "How could I not love you back? You're a sensitive, caring man who feels as passionately about his family as his work."

"And you. Don't forget that."

Heedless of her sticky blouse, Rick pulled her closer. She stood on tiptoe, and this time her lips met his first.

"Ahem."

They broke apart, and with guilty expressions, turned.

Graham shook his head. "Dad, you'd give me all kinds of trouble if you caught me in a lip lock like that."

Henry rolled down on her heels. Rick cut his eyes at his son, then pulled Henry forward. "Graham, this is Henrietta Steelman."

"Yeah," Graham said, smirking. "*Henry,* right?"

"That's right." Henry smiled and held out her hand. "We met at the door, but how do you do, Graham?"

He stared at her hand in disgust. "Dad said you were the career type."

"Graham!"

Henry lowered her hand. "That's all right, Rick. He's entitled to an opinion."

"But he—"

She turned to Graham. "What do you do for a living, Mr. Montgomery?"

"Come on. I go to high school."

"Then think about how hard it is for your dad to keep your household together. He has a career. I have a career. We work to take care of our families."

"I have a job," Graham said defensively. "I work in Dad's office during the summer."

"I'm glad to hear it." She gestured at the sophisticated decor. "You have a good life here, Graham. A lot of people are lucky just to have three square meals a day. But don't forget your father works hard to earn his money. Just like I work to support my family."

"Henry's very talented at what she does," Rick said. "It would be a shame to hide that light under a bushel."

His words softened and swelled inside her. "Thank you, Rick."

Graham shifted from one foot to the other. "Yeah, well, if we're done, I'm heading out for the mall."

Rick's face darkened. "No, you're not, young man. I told you this was a special dinner tonight. I want all of you to meet Henry—"

"I met her."

Rick glared. "And get to know her better."

Henry smiled at Graham. "That's all right. I know what it's like when your parents' friends come over and you're expected to visit."

"No," Rick said firmly. "I told him about this, and he will stay to eat."

"Fine." Graham turned on his heel. "But I don't have to like it!"

❧

Rick offered Henry one of his sweatshirts, and she changed in the guest bathroom. As she rinsed her stained blouse in the sink, she eyed the expensive wallpaper, claw-foot tub, plush rug, and brass fixtures. Even the bathroom was more tasteful than her home.

She still chuckled as she emerged into the cool, ivory-painted hallway. Rick waited at the end of the hall, smiling, chef's hat and apron gone.

"I made Graham finish grilling. For punishment." He grinned, encircling her waist with an arm. "Now come meet the rest of the family. I'm sure they'll be more receptive."

"I hope so."

She matched his stride as they passed more ivory walls and the leather furniture in the den. She felt Rick's gaze and glanced up.

"You look very. . .fetching. I don't think I've ever seen my shirt look better."

"What, this thing?" She glanced down at the light blue sweatshirt and celebrity walk-a-thon logo.

"Uh-huh." His gaze flickered over her again, and he

tickled her waist with his fingers.

The back door slammed open, sliding glass protesting in its tracks. "Dad! We need—"

The girl stopped short. Her face changed from excitement to shock. She stared at Henry and Rick then at her father's arm firmly wrapped around Henry's waist.

"Rachel." Rick released Henry and gestured. "This is Mrs. Henrietta Steelman. Henry, this is—"

"Yes. Rachel." Henry stepped forward and extended her hand. "How are you? I've heard so much about you from your father."

Rachel shook Henry's hand without enthusiasm, keeping her gaze downcast. "It's nice to meet you, Mrs. Steelman."

Henry sought to put her at ease. "Please call me Henry."

"Wachel! Wachel!"

Two-year-old Clara toddled through the open door. Clutching a plastic shovel, she was covered with dirt from her baby-fine brown hair to her frilly dress and patent leather shoes. A grin lit her face from ear to ear.

Rachel's expression was contrite. "I'm sorry. I know you wanted Clara all dressed up, but she wanted to play in the flower bed."

Rick laughed and scooped up the dirt-smudged little girl. "That's all right. It's too lovely a January day to worry about nice clothes. Henry, meet my youngest daughter, Clara."

Henry smiled at the glow of adoration in Rick's eyes as he gazed at the little girl. Then she remembered that his wife had died not long after Clara was born. The child must sometimes be a painful reminder, as well.

Henry lifted the little girl's soft, small hand. "Hello, Clara," she murmured.

Clara beamed. "Hey-wo." She stretched out her arms to Henry. "Daddy, cwoser!"

Rick laughed. "Sure thing. Come meet the pretty lady up close."

Clara studied Henry with a child's curiosity, apparently deciding whether to trust this stranger. Henry held her breath, hoping the little girl would rule in her favor. Her arms suddenly ached with the memory of holding a child, and she fleetingly wondered if she might some day have a chance to hold one of her own—a baby—again.

Laughing, Clara stretched out her arms.

With a smile, Rick relinquished the girl, barely able to restrain her from jumping out of his arms.

Henry gently hugged the child. "Will you be my friend, Clara?"

Clara nodded her head solemnly and broke into another smile. Henry hugged her again, then when the girl didn't resist, added a quick kiss on top of her head.

"I think she likes you," Rick said softly. A slow, warm smile spread across his face.

Henry glanced up and caught Rachel's eye. The girl had a sad expression on her face, but her gaze held no malice. Henry thought she saw tears in her eyes, but Rachel swiped her hand quickly across her face.

"Graham says the barbecue's almost ready," she said. "I'll go get John from Timothy's next door, then we'll be ready to eat."

"You already set the table?" Rick shook his head. "I

don't know what I'd do without you, Rachel. You sure keep things humming around here."

Rachel shot Henry another haunted look, then jerked her head. "If you'll excuse me, Henry. . .Dad."

She bolted from the room and out the front door.

Clara cooed, entranced with Henry's dangling gold earrings. With a puzzled expression, Rick turned back. "What got into Rachel?"

Henry sighed. "The same thing that's wrong with Graham, evidently. They know how much you like me, and they see me as a threat."

"A threat to what?"

Clara laughed as she swung Henry's earring back and forth.

"A threat to the memory of their mother," Henry said softly.

Rick laughed. "That's ridiculous! You couldn't replace Nancy. You're nothing like her!"

Henry winced, hoping her face didn't reveal how much his words stung. He made it sound as though she couldn't measure up.

She set Clara down, and the little girl toddled to the back door. "You should tell all of your children that I have no intention of replacing Nancy," Henry said quietly.

Rick reached for her hand. "I didn't mean anything by that. I certainly didn't mean to imply that you and I . . .that is. . ."

He broke off, his face turning red. "Oh, come on," he mumbled. "Let's go eat."

❧

Henry wiped the last of the sauce from her mouth with a napkin, then leaned back with a contented sigh. "You barbecue some wonderful spareribs, Rick." She glanced across the table. "You, too, Graham." He didn't even look up from his plate.

"It's our specialty," Rick said. "Steaks and chicken are fine for beginners, but it takes a skilled chef to baste the ribs just right, then barbecue them to perfection."

"They were the best, Dad," nine-year-old John piped up. He smiled at Henry, sitting at his side. "Didn't you like the potato salad?"

Henry leaned over, warmed that the boy had taken an instant liking to her the moment they met. "I loved the potato salad," she confessed in a whisper.

"I made it," Rachel said.

Henry smiled. "Will you give me the recipe?"

Rachel shrugged, dropping her gaze to her plate. "I guess."

Silence fell over the table. Henry bit the inside of her lip. Graham had been quiet for the entire meal, sullen, picking at his food. Rachel hadn't contributed much to the conversation, either. Her attitude had been respectful but reserved, as though Henry were a visiting schoolteacher.

John had chattered from the moment they'd met and even taken her by the hand to seat her. He insisted on sitting beside her. Already won over, Clara happily smashed potato salad in her high chair.

"What's for dessert?" Rick rubbed his hands together. "A good meal should always be followed by an even better dessert." He paused. "Didn't Vera Fabbish say that?"

The children giggled. Even Graham cracked a smile. Perplexed, Henry looked from one face to another, waiting for an explanation.

Rick finally stopped chuckling. "Ever since I started the cooking class and Vera found out who my parents were, she's taken it upon herself to visit us regularly. She usually brings a casserole or two as an excuse, but I think she really comes to sit on our sofa and dispense advice."

John's giggles turned into a fit of unbroken laughter. "One day she was wearing shorts and stayed so long, she got stuck to the leather!"

Henry hid a smile behind a hand. Rick gave her a mock stern look, turning the expression on the others. "I thought we agreed we wouldn't discuss. . ." His shoulders shook, and his face twisted with mirth until he gave in to a full-fledged chuckle. "She means well."

Rachel's faint smile faded. "I'll get dessert."

Henry smiled and rose. "Let me help."

"No," Rachel said sharply. She squared her shoulders and lifted her chin as she swept past Henry. "I can manage."

Henry sat back down. Rick flashed her a thankful smile, tempering Rachel's rebuff.

Graham yawned loudly. "Can I go now?"

"But—"

Henry laid a hand on Rick's knee to still his protest. "It's all right," she said softly.

Rick sighed. "Fine, Graham. You may go."

"Thanks." The chrome leg of his chair scraped against the tiled floor as he pushed back and left the room. They heard the front door slam.

Rick's face darkened. "He really should have stayed."

"He's a teenage boy," Henry said softly. "It'd be hard enough for him to sit still if I were even just your business associate."

Rick's eyes gleamed. "I'm glad you're not."

Smiling, Henry shyly turned her face. Rachel entered, her arms laden with a tray full of ice cream and pound cake. She glanced at her father and Henry, then paled.

Clara pounded a fist against her tray. Without a word, Rachel placed a small bowl in front of her. Clara scooped up a frozen lump with her hand, and Rachel silently continued to pass out bowls.

Henry lifted the spoon to her mouth. The frigid ice cream sent a sharp rush to her head and chest, but she swallowed with delight.

"Homemade!" she said when she regained her breath. She smiled at Rachel. "Did you make this yourself?"

Rachel nodded. "It was Mom's favorite. Tutti-frutti."

Henry idly stirred her ice cream. "My husband used to make this a lot, Rachel," she said softly. "It was kind of you to remind me of him, too."

Rachel reddened, then lowered her head until her long hair hid her face.

John stared at Henry's bowl. "Hey! You're making soup!"

Henry smiled, not missing a stroke with her spoon. "I like my ice cream this way. It makes a frosting to drizzle over my slice of cake, you see?"

John peered into her bowl as Henry spooned ice cream on top of her cake. His eyes widened, twinkling. "Neat! I want to try that." He turned to his father. "I hope you bring her home more often."

Rick smiled at her. "I'll do my best."

Henry lingered at the Montgomerys' for another hour. She admired Clara's cheerful nursery, decorated in primary colors and dancing bears. One by one, the little girl pulled toys off a low shelf to play with Henry and Rick. Henry had forgotten how much fun it was to play with a toddler, and several times she again saw a warm light in Rick's eyes when their gazes met over the little girl's head.

Henry grinned at the nuclear fallout sign adorning the closed door to Graham's room. John grabbed her hand and pulled her into his own room, its walls ambiguously covered with ninja character posters and cross-stitched children's verses. He was still at that in-between age, not a little boy anymore, but not yet a teenager.

When Henry politely asked, Rachel somewhat grudgingly showed her room. As tasteful and clean as the rest of the house, it was decorated in matching Victorian prints from the bedspread to the bay window curtains to the wallpaper. Henry recognized the classic mark of a famous British designer.

"What a lovely room, Rachel," she said softly. "I always wanted a cushioned bay window when I was a girl. It seemed like a great place to dream."

"Rachel designed the room herself," Rick said. "We

moved into the house about a year ago."

Henry glanced from the desk to the bed to the dresser. Unlike her own room, there wasn't a sign of clutter anywhere. "You're a very tidy person," she said with a smile.

Rachel shrugged, eyes downcast, as she fiddled with the doorknob on the closet door. "I like things to be neat, but Mrs. Brewster does most of the cleaning."

"Mrs. Brewster?"

"The maid," Rick said. "She comes at least once a week. Sometimes twice."

Henry said her good-byes to Rachel then stuck her head in John's room. He and Clara were absorbed in a mock battle of plastic figures. They both returned her farewell hastily, then went back to play.

Rick put an arm around her and led her to the front door. He handed her a plastic bag with her soiled blouse. "I'm sorry I ruined it."

"That's all right." She twisted the plastic ends into a knot and bit her lip. "You never told me you had a maid."

"Does it matter?"

"Well. . .yes. You didn't seem too pleased when I told you I was thinking about getting one."

Rick sighed, spreading his hands out wide. "Henry, I have four children."

"And I have two. Do maids have a minimum offspring requirement for their employers?"

"No, but. . ." He broke off, letting his hands drop helplessly.

"But I'm a woman," she finished. "Is that it? I'm

supposed to not only know how to run a house but enjoy doing it?"

He sighed again, looking sheepish. "No, I guess not. I've worked with women on a professional level and never thought about it before. The women I've known on a personal level were all homemakers. By choice."

"This one isn't," Henry said, slightly miffed.

Rick stepped forward, pulling her into a warm embrace. "Right now all I know is that I'm in love with you, and you're in love with me. That ought to be enough to make up for a multitude of differences."

Henry closed her eyes as his lips covered hers, but her heart quivered. Even if Rick wanted her in his life and could overlook what he perceived as shortcomings, two of his four children couldn't.

nine

Mary Alice stared as she shoveled pasta into her mouth. Henry set down her own fork, smiling. "What? Do I have tomato sauce on my face?"

"Mmmff," Mary Alice mumbled, swallowing furiously. "You just look different. I can't get over it. You're glowing. And you've given up those uptight businesswoman's suits."

Henry glanced down. "This *is* a suit."

Mary Alice took a final swallow, then a drink of water. "Yes, but it's much more feminine than what you used to wear. Instead of black and gray, you're wearing real colors. Red. . .blue. . .green. . .happy colors."

She sat back in her chair and folded her arms. "You're in love!"

"Shh!" Henry brushed a finger against her own lips, certain that her sister's voice had carried halfway across the Italian restaurant. "Why didn't you just go on television and announce it?"

"I knew it!" Mary Alice's eyes shone as she leaned forward. "Come on. Tell me all about it."

"There's nothing to tell." Henry picked up her fork and poked at her spaghetti to avoid her sister's gaze. "Rick and I enjoy each other's company. That's all."

"Uh-huh." Mary Alice smirked. "Come on, Henry. This is your little sister here! The one you used to tell about each and every one of your boyfriends!"

Henry glanced up. "This is different. With Les, I knew it was the real thing. But now I'm older and not so certain."

"It was Vera Fabbish," Mary Alice said, nodding. "Didn't I tell you that woman would throw you two together?"

Henry smiled. "I don't know if she can take all the credit, but she's certainly done her best."

"So when's the wedding?"

"Mary Alice!" Henry struggled to cover a smile at the thought. "Rick and I have only known each other a few months. You're being a bit hasty, don't you think?"

"It's never too early, especially if you want a June wedding. That's only four months away. And as your future matron of honor, let me warn you that I have a busy schedule."

"Oh, really!" Henry dipped her fork to twirl the pasta, then shoved it in her mouth to avoid further conversation. Common sense ruled that her sister was premature in her speculations, but a portion of Henry's heart longed for a storybook ending.

She swallowed quickly, glancing at her watch. "Look at the time! I've got to get back to work by one o'clock or Mr. Fitzhugh will fire me. I've taken on three extra estates just this week. I think that man is trying to overload me with work. Instead of dangling that vice presidency, I think he's secretly hoping I'll quit."

"Why don't you?" Mary Alice shrugged, a gleam in her eye. "When you marry Mr. Famous Architect, you won't have to work."

"Not you, too!" Henry groaned. She fished in her purse for her wallet and tossed some bills at her sister. "Be a lamb and take care of the bill, will you? I've got a five-block walk back to the office."

"Sure, sure." Mary Alice smiled. "You'd better practice walking, all right. You'll need it when you walk down that long aisle at church."

Henry flashed her sister a look of exasperation then headed for the door.

🍃

Pastor Oliver Reynolds smiled at the group assembled around him on folding chairs in the fellowship hall. Rick squeezed Henry's hand. They smiled at each other, remembering the New Year's Eve party.

"I think everybody's here, Oliver," Vera said. She took a seat beside the pastor.

"Good." Once again, he beamed at the group of twenty. "Thank you all for giving up a week night to meet here to plan the Bread and Fish program."

"It's about time we got this thing going," Vera said, nodding. "This community needs more than the soup kitchen can provide."

"Exactly. So what we propose is to work out a food distribution program to take directly to the people. What that involves is up to the people in this room."

A young woman from Rick and Henry's cooking class raised a hand. "Does it have to be hot meals?"

"It could be," Oliver said. "Or it could be canned goods delivered on a regular basis. That's what we're here to decide."

"Maybe we should start by placing someone in

charge," Vera suggested.

"That's a great idea," Oliver said. "I'll be on hand to help out in any way, but we need a leader."

Vera rose to her feet. "I nominate Henrietta Steelman."

An approving murmur rippled through the crowd. Henry blinked. "Me?"

Rick squeezed her hand. "Why not?" he whispered. "You'd be great at it."

Oliver raised a hand to quiet the room. "Anybody else have a nomination or want to volunteer to head the program?"

Silence.

Lowering his hand, Oliver smiled at Henry. "Looks like you're elected." He stood and gestured at his chair. "Come on up here and take charge. I'm just an interested observer from now on."

Embarrassed, Henry cast a quick glance at Rick. He gave her a warm smile of reassurance, and she took the empty chair.

Vera leaned forward. "I know you can do it, dear." She winked.

"Well. . ." Henry gazed out at the faces. Some she knew and some she didn't. What should she say?

She straightened her shoulders. This was just another business delegation. And for a good cause, too.

"All right," she said warmly, feeling the keen sense of responsibility. "The first thing we need to do is decide how we want to operate. I'm sure we all have our individual ideas, but let's make the discussion as brief as possible. As I see it, we can either deliver groceries, prepared meals, or a combination of both."

"Meals on Wheels already delivers hot meals," Rick said. "We might just be duplicating their service."

"Good point," Henry said, furrowing her brow. "And the plus side for groceries is that it would be more a matter of money than manpower." She grinned. "If you'll pardon the expression, ladies."

The room laughed. Henry rubbed her hands together, excited. Leadership was one of her strong points, and she hadn't had a chance to use that gift in her church. She enjoyed assigning tasks by ability and giving the individual creative freedom to solve the dilemma. Nothing gave her greater pleasure than to see the pride on someone else's face from a job well done.

"Excuse me."

A woman timidly raised her hand at the back of the room. She stood up slowly, and a shy smile etched its way across her face. "I'm Polly Faradon. I. . .I'm new to this church."

"She works in the soup kitchen," Vera said. "Jumped right in from the first day she joined the church."

Henry smiled at the pleasant-looking blond, judging her to be in her mid- to late twenties. "What's your idea, Polly?"

Polly cleared her throat, glancing nervously around the room. "As Mrs. Fabbish says, I work in the soup kitchen occasionally, and a lot of times there's food left over. Sometimes we use it the next day, sometimes not. Couldn't we use some of the food we prepare in the church for this program? And besides," she continued in a rush, "I, uh, like to cook. I'd hate to just shell out money or shop at the grocery store. I'd much rather make something and take it in person."

Rick nodded. "A serving heart," he murmured as Polly hastily took her seat.

Henry pushed down a twinge of guilt. The woman did have a point. "Polly, make a list for the next few days and see what kind of food we have left over from the soup kitchen. Also, work on some ideas for what we could prepare, either here at the church or in our own homes. I'll work on a budget and securing funds."

Mind racing, she closed her eyes in concentration. "Hmm. Let's divide into two teams. Those who are more interested in cooking can work with Polly. Everybody else can work with me. We'll get someone to work with both teams." She opened her eyes. "Vera?"

"I'd better work with Polly, dear. I know that kitchen pretty well. I wouldn't be much good at raising money."

Henry glanced at the other faces, then her gaze fell on Rick. "How about you?" she asked. "You've even spent more time in the kitchen lately thanks to the cooking class."

Rick laughed along with the rest of the room. "I'd be honored to accept the position as committee liaison," he said, bowing his head as though receiving knighthood.

"Good. That's settled," Henry leaned back, pleased. Things were progressing even better than she'd expected. With a little dedication, they'd have this program up and running in no time.

As Henry asked for volunteers to work with Polly, Rick smiled and winked at her. Her heart warmed, and she looked forward to the coming days. Not only would she be able to serve the community through the Bread and Fish program, she would also have another excuse to spend time with Rick.

☙

Clayton Fitzhugh tapped a finger against one stack of several folders lining Henry's desk like an ancient city wall. "Why aren't these done?"

Henry glanced up, hoping her eyes didn't appear as red as they felt. She'd stayed up late last night, trying to catch up on work. "I'll be finished with them before lunch, Mr. Fitzhugh."

His eyes narrowed. "Hmmph! You'd better!"

The door banged shut behind him. Henry was certain she saw the window vibrate.

She closed the folder she'd been working on and set it aside. Pulling another one from the stack, she glanced at the desk clock. Eleven o'clock. Judging from the work yet to accomplish, lunch wouldn't come for another four hours.

Reaching for the telephone, she rubbed the bridge of her nose. Henry cradled the receiver against a shoulder with her chin, smothering a yawn as she dialed.

"Rick Montgomery."

"Hi," she managed to say before she smothered another yawn in her palm.

Rick laughed. "Am I keeping you awake?"

"No." She frowned, irritated. Did he have to joke? "I can't make lunch today."

Rick groaned. "But we were going to talk about Bread and Fish!"

"I know that," she said sharply, tapping a pencil

against her desk. Relenting, she softened her tone. "How about tonight?"

"Tonight I'm getting together with Polly Faradon. She and I are supposed to hammer out some details."

"Well, there's always class tomorrow night." Henry skeptically flipped through her daily planner. "No, wait. I have to meet with a customer. I can't even come to class."

Rick groaned again. "Henry, we have to get serious about this program. It's never going to get off the ground if we don't get everything straight."

Henry curled her fingers around the edge of her desk. "I realize that," she said in a low voice. "I'm trying to make time. Look, I've been meaning to get you and your kids over to meet my kids. Why don't you all come for dinner Saturday night? The kids can get acquainted, and we can talk about the program over dessert."

"Well. . ."

Despite her edginess, her lips curved in a smile. "Is it my cooking you're worried about?"

"Actually, I was thinking about the kids. If your children are as standoffish as mine have been lately, we're in for an interesting evening."

Henry smothered another yawn. She couldn't remember the last time she'd said more than a few words to her kids.

"Both Brian and Cindy *have* seemed out of sorts. I hadn't noticed until you mentioned it just now, but they haven't been their usual selves. Brian's been even moodier than normal."

"He hasn't been very pleasant when I've come to pick you up. I think he's having the same reservations about me that my kids seem to have about you."

"But Cindy? I thought she liked you."

"Even she's seemed cool to me the last few weeks."

Henry rested her chin over the mouthpiece and closed her eyes. What more, Lord? Work was a shambles, her family had turned into strangers, the food distribution was lagging behind in schedule. . .

"Henry? Are you still there?"

She smiled. "Just barely."

Rick laughed softly. "After dinner tonight, take a hot bubble bath and forget about everything for at least an hour. Promise?"

"Promise." Henry smiled. "What would I do without you in my life, Rick Montgomery?"

"Someday soon I hope you'll be wondering what to do with me in your life," he said. "Permanently."

Henry let the implication set in. "Do you mean that?" she whispered.

"Yes, Henry," he said in a deep voice. "I'll call you later tonight. After the kids have gone to bed and you've had your bath."

Henry felt a shiver course up her spine. "Okay," she whispered. "Bye."

She replaced the receiver, then turned back to the folders.

≈

That night after a long soak in the tub, Henry got ready for bed and decided to study her Bible while she waited for Rick's call. Remembering his words from the morning, her mind wandered to the proverb about the excellent wife. No doubt Rick had read that passage, too.

Henry frowned as she studied. The unnamed biblical woman seemed like some sort of Super Mom: She spun wool, searched for food, rose early in the morning to feed her household, and worked until late at night. She also helped the poor, sewed her own clothes, sold her handmade garments and belts, spoke words of wisdom, taught kindness, and never had a spare moment. And because of this, her children and her husband praised her name.

"Whew!" Henry marked her place with a finger and closed the book. "Talk about your Type-A personalities. Nobody can live up to that!"

She leaned back against the propped-up pillows and glanced over at the phone, then at the clock. Eleven-thirty. Rick should have phoned by now.

"He and Polly must have gotten into a good discussion," she mumbled, sliding down against the pillows. She yawned, covering her mouth with a fist. She barely had the energy to set the Bible aside and turn out the light before her eyes closed.

Just before she fell asleep, she had a fleeting image of the excellent wife. And for some reason, the woman seemed very shy and had blond hair.

ten

Mary Montgomery set down her china cup. "I'm glad you could meet me for lunch, Henry."

"Thank you for inviting me." Henry glanced around the elegant tearoom, located in one of Houston's finer hotels. A string quartet played softly in the corner, and dutiful, hushed waiters attended wealthy diners at pale-covered tables.

She sighed. "It's good to get away from the office."

"Rick said you'd been spending an inordinate amount of time working lately. Are you sure you want to have him and the children for dinner on Saturday? They're quite a crew to cook for." She leaned forward, whispering, "Not to mention, if you're like me, I always leave the housecleaning until the last minute!"

Henry chuckled and Mary straightened with a smile. "That's better, dear. You've been so somber all through lunch. Is something troubling you?"

Henry lowered her gaze to her linen napkin. She brushed a soft edge with a fingernail, hesitating.

"Henry? What's wrong?"

Henry met Mary's gaze. "Tell me about Nancy."

Mary looked puzzled. "What do you want to know, dear?"

"What she was like. Was she funny? Was she serious? Did she dress in the latest fashion? Did she prefer butterscotch or chocolate topping on her ice cream?"

"In other words, everything."

"Yes."

Mary smiled sadly. "Nancy was a sweet, cheerful girl when she married Rick, and she grew into a lovely, generous woman. Taking care of her home and family was second only to her faith."

"But she never worked outside of the home?"

"Not for money. But after John started kindergarten, she volunteered extensively."

Henry twisted her napkin around a finger. "Rick's home is very important to him, isn't it? It's immaculate."

Mary's lips twisted in a wry grin. "A little too immaculate, if you ask me. He may have a maid to pick up after everyone, but he's hard on the kids when it comes to taking care of that showplace. Nancy appreciated her lovely home, but she wanted it to be comfortable. Livable."

Mary laid a gentle hand on Henry's arm. "Why all the questions?"

Henry drew a deep breath. "Rick and I are. . .talking seriously about our relationship."

Mary's face filled with joy. "I'm so pleased. You strike me as a perfect match for Rick."

"Wait a minute. You sound like my sister." Henry grinned. "We haven't actually said anything about marriage. I've got a career to manage, and I'm not sure if I'm the type of woman who's wanted by Rick and his kids."

Mary smiled sympathetically. "God made us all different but equal, Henry. I'm surprised a woman of your independence and confidence would even question your worth."

"It's not that," Henry said, searching for words. "I know what my strengths are. . .as well as my weaknesses."

She shifted in her chair. "Les. . .that was my husband. . .he loved and accepted me for who I was. Not for who he wanted me to be. He teased me about my klutziness around the kitchen and the house, but he also was my biggest cheerleader. He was content for me to have the limelight, so to speak, while he took care of things in the background."

"And Rick?"

Henry laughed. "Rick admires me, too, because we're so much alike. We're both ambitious go-getters. As long as we're dating, it's all right. But if we were married . . .Well, I wonder how content he would be to have a wife out front with him. A wife with a hectic schedule. After all, we'd have six children in our family."

Mary shook her head, casting Henry a stern look. "Don't change a thing about yourself. You're wonderful just the way you are. Rick thinks so, too. Love always finds a way."

Henry grinned, feeling optimistic again. "I hope so."

❧

Brian looked up the number of the maid who'd cleaned the house for the past few weeks, then dialed. It was a shame she didn't speak English. None of the Steelmans spoke much Spanish, but Mrs. Maldonado had come highly recommended. Rick Montgomery usually came over when there was interpreting to do.

He spoke Spanish.

Brian tapped his foot until the other end of the telephone line clicked. "Uh, *Señora* Maldonado? Uh, *soy* Brian Steelman." He made a face, holding the excited chatter from the other end of the phone away from his ear. "*Sí. El hijo de Señora* Steelman. Um, *mi madre. . . dice. . .no venga la casa en el sabado. ¿Porqué?* Why doesn't she want you to come?"

Brian hastily filtered through the limited Spanish he'd acquired from the classroom and playground to come up with an excuse.

"She's sick! Yeah, she's, uh. . .*mi madre está. . . .*" What was the word for sick? *Em, en,* something. What had Chuy Mendoza said when his mother was ordered to bed?

"*¡Encinta!* That's it! *¡Mi madre está encinta!*"

He heard a pause on the other end of the line, then a rapid succession of Spanish. Mrs. Maldonado's voice rose to a fevered, imploring pitch. Brian held the phone away from his ear again, grinning at his apparent success. She was probably telling him how sorry she was and recommending a hearty bowl of chicken soup or something.

"Uh, *Señora* Maldonado. I have to go. Uh, *gracias. Adiós.*"

Brian hung the phone up, silencing the chatter. Feeling smug, he leaned against the desk and folded his arms. "That ought to take care of things."

Cindy walked into the room, Barbie doll and box in hand. "Who were you talking to?"

Brian flashed his sister a self-satisfied smile. "Mrs.

Maldonado. She won't be able to clean house in time for the stupid dinner on Saturday."

"We'd better tell Mom. That's two days from now. Maybe she can find somebody else."

Brian pushed away from the desk. "Don't you get it? If the house is a mess, ol' what's-his-face won't want to marry Mom."

Cindy bit her lip. "She sure does like him, though."

"Oh, come on, Cinder-face," Brian snapped. "Do you want him to replace Dad? Mom doesn't spend enough time with us as it is, what with her job, that cooking class, and that guy. Besides, he's got kids already. Four of 'em! Do you want more brothers and sisters?"

"It might be nice to have a sister," Cindy said wistfully.

"It wouldn't be the same. Listen, don't say anything to Mom about Mrs. Maldonado. Do what I say on Saturday, and that man won't be taking Dad's place, okay?"

Cindy scuffed a toe against the carpet. "Okay," she mumbled. "What do I have to do?"

Brian's grin stretched from ear to ear. "Here's the plan. On Saturday morning you suddenly remember. . ."

Henry stared in disbelief at her daughter. "What do you mean you have to take cookies to a Girl Scout meeting this afternoon? This is Saturday!"

"It's a special cookie contest," Cindy said calmly. "They have to be homemade cookies."

"Sweetheart, couldn't you have remembered yesterday? I planned to be in the kitchen all day cooking for our dinner tonight. Rick and his kids are coming."

Cindy shrugged. "I'm sorry, Mom."

"Can't we just buy some and pretend we made them?" Henry asked, desperate. "I don't have time—"

"I can make them by myself. I'll make sugar cookies. They're easy."

Henry cast a dubious glance at her daughter. "Well, okay. And if you make a mess, Mrs. Maldonado can clean it up when she comes at two o'clock."

"Okay, Mom," Cindy said cheerfully. She moved slowly around the kitchen, taking her time in finding an apron and collecting ingredients.

Henry felt a dull throb in her head. She stared at her watch, tension gnawing her stomach. Eleven o'clock. The Montgomerys were due to arrive at six-thirty. She could start dinner at three o'clock while Mrs. Maldonado finished cleaning up the house. For now, she could clip those hedges out front. She'd been meaning to trim them for a long time, but just hadn't had the time.

She glanced down at her frayed jeans and favorite sweatshirt with its cutoff sleeves. She was certainly dressed to do yard work. As she headed to the garage for the hedge clippers, she smiled. Maybe the outdoor work would relax her.

❧

"Mom!" Brian called out the front door. "Are you ready to take me to Adam's?"

Henry paused with hedge clippers in hand, then wiped her forehead with her wrist. "Adam's? I don't remember anything about your going to his house today."

"I told you several days ago."

"But he lives across town! It'll take an hour to get there and back. Not to mention picking you up." Henry sighed, shoulders sagging. "All right. Come on."

An hour later, Henry winced as she passed the shrubs while pulling the car into the driveway. The hedge was horribly lopsided where she'd stopped working. She glanced at the car's clock as she eased into the garage. One o'clock. Thankfully Mrs. Maldonado would be here soon.

"Cindy, I'm home," she announced as she entered the kitchen. "How did your—what happened in here?"

Henry stood stock-still, surveying the empty kitchen. Sugar littered the floor like sawdust, and dripping water formed a sticky puddle below the silverware drawer. Flour dusted the counters, and chocolate chips dotted the kitchen floor like a Hansel and Gretel trail.

"Cynthia Renee Steelman!" Henry planted her fists on her hips. "You have three seconds to get in here!"

"Coming, Mom," Cindy said meekly, appearing from the bedroom hallway. "I'm cleaning it up. Honest! You should have seen it before."

Henry closed her eyes and let out a long breath. The dull throb in her head had lodged itself directly behind her eyes. "What happened?"

Cindy bowed her head. "I spilled the sugar."

"I see. And the flour?"

"I was lifting the bag from one counter to another, and. . . Well, I didn't know it was already open!"

The pressure behind Henry's eyes increased. "And the chocolate chips?"

"The bag spilled." Cindy looked up hopefully. "You

aren't mad, are you?"

Henry sighed. "No, I'm not mad, honey. Accidents happen. Let's start cleaning up. What we don't finish, Mrs. Maldonado can take care of."

Guilt flashed briefly across Cindy's face, but she quickly turned her head. "Okay, Mom."

They worked for an hour, Henry nervously consulting her watch every five minutes. She wanted everything to be perfect this evening, and so far nothing had gone right.

She left Cindy with the last of the cleanup and wandered the rest of the house taking inventory. Bathtubs with rings, unmade beds, towels thrown everywhere. . . What a wreck. She should clean first so the maid could find room to clean up!

Two-thirty. She frowned. Where was Mrs. Maldonado? It wasn't like her to be late.

The telephone rang. "Don't back out on me, Mrs. Maldonado. Please!" she muttered, then lifted the receiver. "Steelman residence. Henry speaking."

"Mom! Where are you? You're supposed to come get me!"

"Brian!" Henry slumped to her bed, holding her tired head in her hand. "You're ready to come home now? Can't Adam's parents bring you? I'm kind of in a jam here."

"They're going out soon. The other direction from our house."

Henry sighed. "All right. I'll be there as soon as I can."

An hour later they pulled into the driveway. Henry

reminded herself to finish clipping the hedge. It looked as if a dinosaur had taken several bites out of it.

"Why didn't I call a professional?" she berated herself out loud as she got out of the car.

"Oh, yeah." Brian's voice was unusually cheerful. "Speaking of professionals, Mrs. Maldonado called yesterday and said she can't come."

"*What?*" Henry slammed the car door. She winced and closed her eyes against the increased pounding in her head. She lowered her voice. "What do you mean she can't come?"

Brian shrugged and entered the house. "I guess something came up."

Henry stood in the garage, alone. "She can't come today," she whispered. She had the absurd urge to giggle.

"Mom!" Cindy stuck her head through the door. "Are you all right?"

Henry let out a deep breath and pressed her head against her hands. "Sure, sure."

She squared her shoulders. Henry Steelman never gave up. They'd get this house in tip-top order yet!

❧

Rick pulled the minivan up to the curb and shut off the engine. Four pairs of young eyes stared out the windows at the Steelman home.

Graham smirked. "Nice hedges."

"I think they look cool!" John said with awe.

Clara babbled with excitement from her car seat next to a quiet Rachel.

Rick cleared his throat and picked up a spring bouquet

from the seat. "Are we ready?"

A mixed chorus of groans and cheers answered, and then they crossed the distance to the front porch. After he straightened a child's collar here and pressed down a cowlick there, Rick rang the doorbell.

Graham sniffed the air. "Something smells funny."

Rick frowned. Henry had gotten better at her cooking. He'd seen it himself at class. Surely she wouldn't have. . .

The door opened suddenly, and Henry appeared. Rick did a double take. He'd never seen her looking less than professional, but here she was in a cutoff sweatshirt and frayed jeans. Hair straggled limply around her face and shoulders and flour dotted her clothes.

"Come in, come in!" she said with exaggerated cheerfulness. "You'll have to forgive the house. We've had kind of a situation today."

"Hello, Henry." Rick bent to kiss her floury cheek as the children filed solemnly past them into the house. He held up the bouquet. "If you'll bring me a vase, I'll put these in water."

"Sure." Henry looked dazed as she accepted the flowers. "Cindy! Brian! The Montgomerys are here."

She turned back to Rick. "You really will have to forgive the mess. It's been an interesting day."

Graham sidled up to his father. "Dad, the place is a wreck," he said. "You should see."

"I'm sure it's not a wreck. Now apologize."

"No, he's right." Henry took Rick's hand. "Let me show you."

She led him to the kitchen. When she pushed open

the swinging door, his mouth dropped.

Dirty pots and pans lined the counter. A skillet on the stove was filled with grease and what appeared to be the charred remains of chicken drumsticks. A bowl of . . .glop was the only way to describe it, stood sadly next to a blender full of more unidentifiable liquid.

Henry opened the refrigerator and pulled out a covered bowl. "We're having salad for dinner. At least that's something that doesn't have to be cooked."

Brian and Cindy appeared in the kitchen, but hung back. Henry gestured at her children for the benefit of the Montgomerys. "This is Brian and Cindy."

She pointed one at a time to Rick's children. "And this is Graham, Rachel, John, and Clara."

"Hi," Brian and Cindy mumbled together. The Montgomery children continued to stare.

"Take them to your rooms to play," Henry said to her children. "Rick and I need to talk."

Graham and Rachel led the way, John and Clara trailing behind. Graham shook his head, letting out a long whistle as he eyed the kitchen. "You two better do more than talk."

"That's enough, Graham," Rick said sternly. He watched them file past, waiting until they were out of earshot.

Alone at last, he turned to Henry. She clutched the salad like a life preserver, a goofy grin plastered on her face. He gently pried the bowl from her hands and put his arm around her. "What happened?"

"Everything, Rick." She gestured around the shambles of a kitchen. "Cindy had to have cookies, Mrs.

Maldonado didn't show up, Brian had to go across town. I didn't have enough time to cook the food, trim the hedges. . ."

"Whoa! Sounds like you've had a busy day."

"I have," she said in a small voice.

Rick stared down at her face, disturbed to see her lips tremble. Not once had he seen her come close to crying. Not even on the anniversary of Les's death.

He wrapped his arm around her. "It's all right. We'll clean it up together."

"That's the problem," she murmured. "Someone's always having to help with my messes." Her shoulders shook and tears welled in her eyes. "This house business is just too much for me to handle."

Rick drew her against him, suppressing a smile. "It's just been a bad day, Henry. We'll both have lots more of them. Let's order some Chinese food and forget it."

He broke the embrace to tip her face up for a kiss, but she pulled away and reached under the sink for a rag and the spray cleaner.

&

Brian switched on his radio to an alternative rock station. He wasn't too fond of the noise, but he figured Graham Montgomery, being older, would approve. He didn't want to catch any flak. Brian was feeling so guilty, he just wanted to be left alone.

Graham flopped down in a beanbag chair and pawed through a stack of music magazines. He pulled one out. "You like this group?"

Brian shrugged. "I guess so."

Graham glanced up. "What's eating you? That mess

your mom made?"

"She didn't make it."

"Yeah?" Graham laughed. "Well, who did?"

"I did." Brian's face reddened. "Because of your dad."

Graham stopped laughing. "What's wrong with my dad?"

"I don't want him to be my father!"

"Well, I don't want your mother for my mom, either!"

"Good!"

They glared at each other. An ultra-high guitar riff blared from the speakers. Graham winced. "Can't you change that racket to another station?"

Brian flipped the radio off.

Graham laughed, settling back in the chair. "So tell me how you arranged that fiasco out there."

Brian told him, and Graham nodded grudgingly. "I've pulled some sneaky schemes, and that was pretty good. If I had to have a new brother. . .but I'm not saying I want one. . .you wouldn't be half bad."

"Thanks." Brian warmed at the older boy's approval, feeling some of the sting from his guilt lift.

eleven

Rick and Henry had nearly finished cleaning the counters and dishes when the doorbell rang.

"Must be the Chinese food," Rick said, straightening over the broom. "You'd better help, Henry. There's probably a couple of bags."

She followed, and he opened the door to a short Hispanic woman with snapping eyes. "Mrs. Maldonado! What are you—"

She shook her finger at him, then Henry, and burst into a tirade of Spanish. Henry shrank against the wall. She'd never seen the woman so agitated.

Rick help up his hands. "A little slower, *por favor, Señora* Maldonado. *No comprendo.*"

Mrs. Maldonado continued to babble, gesturing from him to Henry. Rick listened attentively, then burst out laughing.

"What's she saying?" Henry said, bewildered.

Rick laughed so hard that Mrs. Maldonado stopped chattering and stared. He wiped his eyes, the last chuckle fading. "I can't quite make out all the words, but apparently she's either saying that you're a live oak or that you're pregnant."

"Pregnant! *¡Sí! ¡En cinta!*" the woman insisted. Her expression softened, and she clasped her hands together in an imploring gesture. "*Señora, Señor, por* *favor. . .El bebé. . ."*

Her words ran into a babble again. Rick's amusement tapered to a smile, and he put an arm around the woman and murmured softly in Spanish. She glanced at Henry with an expression of relief. "Ah, *Señora, perdóname. Perdóname.*" After one last mortified stare, she backed hastily out of the door.

Henry felt her face warm. "She thought I was pregnant! No wonder she wouldn't come clean today. She thought. . ."

She glanced at Rick, who studiously looked away. "It's all straight now," he mumbled. "Let's get back to the kitchen."

❧

But despite the dismal evening's comic relief, Henry's mood refused to be dispelled. She had wanted the evening to unify the two families, to introduce the children to each other and see if the two households could cement. The day's catastrophes had blunted her optimism, however, and she wished the Montgomerys would go home.

Oddly enough, the children seemed to get along, if not beautifully, at least passably. Rachel, Cindy, and Clara set up a Barbie dream world in Cindy's bedroom, and Henry's heart warmed at the sight of Rick's teenage daughter sprawled on the floor alongside the younger Cindy.

Even Graham and Brian amiably discussed music and cars. Henry didn't hear any more sarcastic cracks from Graham, and once she even caught him looking at her with something like sympathy.

After dinner, the children took over the living room to watch television; Rick and Henry retreated to the kitchen.

"You're awfully quiet tonight," he said as they rinsed dishes. "Are you still upset?"

Henry bent to stack a plate in the dishwasher, then picked off a soft noodle. "I'm just tired," she said. Her head still throbbed.

"We were supposed to talk about the Bread and Fish program tonight."

Henry flipped the dishwasher closed and spun the dial to wash. She folded her arms and leaned against the counter, all business. "Where should we start?"

Rick put his hands on her shoulders and led her to the table. "Sit down first. You look worn out. I'll make some coffee, then we can talk."

She watched him bustle around the kitchen, finding the coffee filters and coffee without any help. He measured the ground beans and poured water to drip.

He smiled at her as he retrieved coffee cups, and she felt her heart do a flip. Their first real conversation had occurred over a cup of coffee, and the smell of hazelnut coffee brewing reminded her of the cozy intimacies of marriage. It was the commonplace things she had loved about being a wife: the first cup of coffee in the morning, the late night conversations about the kids. . .even the arguments over the monthly bills.

She turned her head, eyes misting.

Rick set a steaming cup in front of her then peered at her face. "Are you crying?"

She blinked the tears to the back of her eyes. "No."

Rick sat across the table, then took her hand. "What's wrong?"

"It's nothing." Forcing a smile, she lifted the cup to her mouth to hide her face. "Tell me about your meeting with Polly."

Rick set his cup down, all smiles. "That woman is a wonder. She's a whiz with the leftover food from the soup kitchen, and she has the best decorated apartment I think I've ever seen. She has excellent taste."

Henry's hands tightened around the cup. "You went to her apartment?"

"Vera went with me." He quickly swallowed his coffee. "Polly has some good ideas for the program. She wants to start a knitting group to make afghans and scarves. She also volunteered to head up a group to tidy houses. Cleaning, painting, stuff like that."

"Those are good ideas," Henry said in a small voice.

"And she sews, too. She makes the cutest baby clothes. She showed me some she'd made for her niece, and . . .where are you going?"

Henry turned back, hardly aware she'd gotten to her feet. "Bathroom," she mumbled. "Why don't you check on the kids?"

She made her way down the hall to her bathroom, at the far end of the house, then locked the door and collapsed on the chenille mat. She leaned against the cold tile wall and pulled her knees to her chest. Wrapping her arms around her legs, she rested her forehead against her knees.

She wouldn't cry. . .she wouldn't.

How foolish she'd been to think she could juggle her

family, her job, community service, and a man in her life. She felt like one of the kids' old rubber dolls whose arms and legs could be stretched to unreasonable lengths before snapping back.

Or breaking.

Soft knuckles rapped at the door. "Mom?" Brian said in an anxious voice. "Are you okay?"

Henry raised her still-dry face, sighing. She couldn't hide in the bathroom like a child. She'd have to untangle the knotted yarn of her life later.

"I'm fine," she said, rising. "I'll be out in a minute."

"Okay." Brian didn't sound reassured, but Henry heard his carpet-muffled footsteps retreat down the hall.

She glanced at herself in the mirror, groaning at her puffy eyes and red nose. A lot of good it had done to suppress the urge to cry. Except for the lack of tears, she looked as if she'd been bawling her eyes out.

After splashing on cold water, Henry dried her face. She examined herself in the mirror and groaned again. Her face looked better, but now the grungy sweatshirt and blue jeans drew her attention. What a sight she must have been when she opened the door to the Montgomerys!

Feeling guilty for abandoning her company for so long, she quickly changed into a pair of black leggings and a baggy sweater. She pulled her hair back with a barrette and applied fresh makeup.

"Well!" Rick's gaze swept appreciatively over her when she reappeared in the kitchen. "You must be feeling better."

"A little," she admitted.

Laughter erupted from the living room over the

sound of a board game in progress.

"It's amazing." Rick shook his head. "I never would have thought it possible so early, but the kids seem to have hit it off." He paused. "Brian was concerned about you, though. He came in here looking like he wanted to talk to you about something."

Henry frowned. "He didn't say anything."

Rick glanced at the living room, then smiled. His eyes gleamed, and his voice was soft as he took her hand. "Come on, Henry. The kids are busy. Let's sit in the den for a while. Just the two of us."

Henry swallowed. Funny how Rick made her feel like a teenage girl who wanted to hide with her boyfriend from her parents. He made her forget she was supposed to be the parent. "If one of the kids came in, what would they think?"

He smiled, drawing her closer. "They'd think the truth. That I'm crazy in love with you. And they'd know it was true because I would be kissing you. Like this."

He curved a palm under her jaw and bent to kiss her. His lips brushed hers gently, testing, then became more insistent, more passionate.

It was foolish. She didn't have time for romance. And their relationship couldn't possibly work. If they married, they would have six children to raise. *Six?* She couldn't take care of two! Rick might forgive her for one night of bedlam, but not a lifetime. He couldn't see down the road to the endless piles of dirty laundry, messy kitchens, and ruined meals.

She broke away, breathless. "I. . .I think maybe you'd better go."

A slow, teasing smile spread across his face. "Do you think so?"

"Y-yes." She forced herself to turn away. "I'm glad things went well with Polly. Let me know what else happens, all right?"

She could feel his stare like heat on her back. "Henry, what's wrong tonight? Why are you giving me the rush? The kids are quiet, we've already talked about the ministry. . .This should be our time." She felt his hands on her arms. "Our time to dream. There's so much I want to say."

Henry closed her eyes against temptation. "It's been a long day. Thank you for coming over. And for the flowers."

He sighed. "All right, Henry. I'll round up the kids and head out. Then you can get a good night's rest."

"Rest. Sure," she said vacantly, tilting her cheek to accept a final peck. "That's all I need."

❧

The casters on Mr. Fitzhugh's chair squeaked as he leaned forward. Evidently trying to draw out the moment and make Henry squirm, he drummed his fingers against his leather desk blotter and squinted.

Like some sort of self-satisfied toad, Henry thought, fighting the urge to smile. Instead, she lifted her chin, her regal posture a result of childhood ballet lessons. The business world set great store by body language, and she knew all the tricks.

"Well?" he barked, evidently tired of the show-down. "Do you think there's any reason to justify your secretary's behavior?"

Henry clenched her fists in her lap where Mr. Fitzhugh couldn't see them. "Louise is a top-rate secretary," she said firmly. "I gave her permission to take the afternoon off because her little boy was ill."

"*You* gave her permission?"

"Yes, sir. She's under my direct supervision. As are several other people in this department." Henry paused, taking courage. "That's what you hired me to do."

"A decision I've had occasion to question, especially since I have my eyes open for a new vice president." He cleared his throat and shuffled several folders. "I'll let this indiscretion pass this once, but next time I won't be so lenient."

Henry took little satisfaction in her own reprieve. "And Louise?"

Mr. Fitzhugh leveled cold, fathomless eyes. "She's cleaning out her desk."

Henry jumped to her feet. "Sir, I—"

"That will be all," he said, handing her the folders. "I suggest you call a temporary agency until you can find a suitable replacement."

"Louise is the best secretary in the office. If you fire her—"

I said, *"That will be all."*

Henry wavered, pressing the folders between her arm and body to keep her hands from shaking. How dare he! How *could* he!

She clenched her teeth. Nothing she could say would get Louise's job back, and Henry needed that vice presidency for her own security. "Yes, sir," she said, then turned on her heel.

Outside his office, she leaned against the wall, collecting energy. Tears stung the back of her eyes at the thought of the young mother without a job. Would her husband have to leave graduate school to support his family?

Louise walked toward her, a cardboard box cradled in her arms. She smiled bleakly.

"I'm so sorry," Henry said. "I feel like this is all my fault. I should have known Fitzhugh would get angry if you left early."

Louise shuffled the box to one arm and laid a hand on Henry's shoulder. She cast a furtive glance at Mr. Fitzhugh's office. "To tell you the truth," she whispered, "I'm glad it happened. I don't want to work for a man who puts business over family. And something will come up. God will provide for us."

Henry put an arm around her to give her a hug. "You have my number, Louise. Call me if you need anything. Anything at all. I'd be glad to give you a recommendation."

Louise smiled. "Thanks."

Henry helped Louise distribute the box more evenly in her arms. "You've been a great secretary. . .and a good friend."

Louise's smile widened. "You, too. I'll be praying for you and Mr. Montgomery."

Henry's heart sank at the mention of Rick. She forced a smile, then trudged down the hall.

"Henrietta?"

She turned back. Louise was smiling warmly. "Don't ever forget that a family's love is a precious treasure."

Henry nodded and returned to her office.

twelve

Cindy and Brian worked silently at the couch, folding clean laundry to the shrill noise of an early evening game show. Neither cast a glance at the television or each other but concentrated on rolling socks and stacking T-shirts.

Cindy sat down, sighing. "When did Mom say she'd be home? I'm starving!"

"She said she'd be home by six." Brian grimaced, glancing at the clock on the VCR. "It's already past six-thirty now."

The phone rang and he lifted the receiver. "Hello? Oh hi, Mom."

Cindy straightened over the clean piles and clutched a stack of T-shirts.

"Okay," Brian said, rolling his eyes. "We'll watch for her. . .Yeah, I love you, too." He replaced the receiver then kicked the sofa.

Deflated, Cindy slumped. "She's not coming for a while, is she?"

Brian turned back to the laundry, automatically stacking clothes according to owner. "Aunt Mary Alice is going to bring us something to eat."

"*Again?*" Cindy pounded her fist against a stack of clothes. "Why can't we have a mom who stays at home? Or at least a mom who *comes* home?"

"Be quiet, Cinder-face."

"You and your stupid plan to keep her away from Mr. Montgomery. He may not be Dad, but at least if she married him, she might be home once in a while. And I liked Rachel. She was nice to me! She said she liked me, too!"

Cindy snatched up her clothes and fled from the living room. Brian grabbed the clothes he'd folded and followed in the wake of his sister.

"Yeah. Me and my stupid plan," he mumbled.

❧

Rick paused, and Henry's fingers tightened around the phone receiver. She could imagine the look on his face.

"You can't come to class tonight, Henry? That makes . . .how many weeks in a row?"

She sighed. "I know. I don't like it, either. I miss Vera and everybody else."

"How about me? You won't go anywhere with me, and you haven't even called in the last few days."

Henry blinked, swiveling in her chair as though she were avoiding his face. "I'm sorry. It's just that Mr. Fitzhugh has been breathing down my neck, and with Louise gone, there's been even more work to do. I have to work hard so I'll be in the running for a promotion. You know that."

She heard Rick sigh. "Henry, exactly how much does a vice presidency mean to you?"

"How can you ask that?" she said, hurt. "I need to get ahead so I can raise my family. You know how work is. You have to work hard to get ahead."

"But there has to be a line somewhere."

She pressed her thumb against a pencil. "I can't

worry about some imaginary line. I have a job to do." She drew a deep breath. "You're just angry because I haven't had time for you lately."

"How much time have you had for Cindy and Brian?" he countered. "I'll bet you've been neglecting them, too."

The pencil snapped in her hand. "That's none of your business. I can't help that I'm a single mother and have to spend a lot of time with my work. Lots of women do it."

"But you don't have to," he said softly. "You could give it up today, Henry. Our kids seem to get along, and you know I love you."

"Business is my world, Rick," she murmured. "I'm secure here. Not with the washing machine and dishwasher stuff at home."

"You could learn. Nancy always said running a house was just like running a business only much more rewarding."

Henry laughed. "Shuffling dirty laundry, cleaning out bathtubs, and cooking dinner? There's no monetary compensation for that."

Rick was silent a moment. "Some things you do just out of love, Henry. You ought to know that."

Henry cleared her throat. "Look, Rick. All this talk isn't getting my work done, and I have a dinner appointment with a customer."

"Dinner? You're not even eating with your kids?"

She bristled. "This is the only time I have. I'll be home later to help them with their schoolwork."

"Sure, Henry," Rick said, then let out what sounded like a frustrated breath. "I'll give your regards to Vera at class. Why don't you call me later tonight after the kids go to bed? We can talk some more."

"I don't think I'll have time," she said curtly. "Goodbye, Rick."

She set the receiver down without waiting for a reply, then put her head in her hands.

❧

Henry bustled into the exclusive restaurant, checking her watch for the umpteenth time. Traffic had been terrible. As her car crept through the congestion, she'd wondered where everyone else was going. Were they on their way home to family? Off on a date? Or maybe, like she, they had business.

"Business," she mumbled under her breath, glancing at the lush surroundings. "This is a place for people in love, not for people to discuss an estate!"

"Mrs. Steelman?"

Henry turned. A slight, white-haired woman with a warm, wrinkled smile stood beside her. Henry automatically held out her hand for a proper greeting and put on her professional face. "How do you do, Mrs. Smithwick?"

Mrs. Smithwick clasped Henry's hand with both of hers, disdaining protocol. "I've secured us a lovely table over here, my dear. And I hope you don't mind, but I took the liberty of ordering coq au vin for us both. I'm sure you don't want to spend an evening with an old woman."

Nonplussed, Henry followed the woman's lead to a secluded corner table and took a seat. "Sorting through an estate so soon after your husband's death is a painful process, Mrs. Smithwick. We'll spend as much time as necessary."

Mrs. Smithwick smiled patiently as though Henry were a rambling child. "What about you, dear? Won't Mr. Steelman miss you at dinner tonight?"

"My husband is dead, Mrs. Smithwick, which is why I understand how important estates are. It's terrible to have to—"

Mrs. Smithwick leaned forward and covered Henry's hands with her own. "I'm so sorry. And you're so young. Were you fortunate enough to have children?"

"Why, yes. But about your—"

"And how old are they?" Mrs. Smithwick folded her hands in front of her.

"Brian is thirteen and Cindy is eight." Henry cleared her throat. "Now, if you'll—"

"But why aren't you home with them, dear? We could have met any time at your office or in my home. Don't you want to be with your children?"

Henry leaned back, sighing. Why did everyone seem to question her love for her kids? Couldn't they see she was just doing her job? Just trying to make a living?

"Mrs. Smithwick," she tried again, shifting in her chair as though digging in for battle. "My children are quite capable of taking care of themselves for a few hours. And we're here to talk about your husband's estate. Not my personal life."

"Nonsense!" Mrs. Smithwick waved a hand. "I insist you go home right now. We can talk later. My only problem is deciding what to do with my money. My husband left me far too much for my own good."

Henry smothered a grin. Never had she heard any of her customers complain about being left too much money. "Maybe you could start a foundation," she suggested. "Perhaps distribute a regular amount to the charities of your choice."

"A wonderful idea!" Mrs. Smithwick's face lit up. "Just wonderful! You must be a woman who's interested in charities herself."

Henry cringed inwardly, remembering the Bread and Fish program. She hadn't given it much attention lately. "As a matter of fact, my church is starting a food outreach program. I'm the coordinator and in charge of raising money. Would you be interested in hearing more about the program and consider making a donation?"

Mrs. Smithwick's eyes warmed, and she patted Henry's hand. "That's a good girl. I prefer to talk about what I can do with Robert's money rather than the amount. But let's meet another time, shall we? You've already sold me on the idea. I just need to hear the details and write you a check."

Henry smiled, relaxing. "Thank you, Mrs. Smithwick. I'd be grateful to meet another day."

"Call me Mildred, dear. And scoot on home."

Henry gathered her purse then rose. "But what about the dinner? You said you'd already ordered."

"Don't worry about that." Mildred winked. "I'm a big eater."

Henry laughed. The woman couldn't weigh a hundred pounds. "All right, Mrs. . .Mildred," she amended. "May I call you tomorrow to arrange another meeting?"

"I'll be delighted to hear from you again." She waved her hands. "Now shoo!"

❧

Spurred by Mildred's comments, Henry determined not

to miss another dinner because of work. She discovered that if she got to the office by six o'clock, she could leave at five. She also wanted to renew her efforts at the Bread and Fish program and get back to the cooking class.

A day before the next class, she and Rick drove to Polly Faradon's apartment to discuss her group's efforts. The program was near completion, and Henry was excited about seeing it in action.

She also hadn't seen Rick all weekend, due to the volume of work she'd taken home, but they'd talked several times on the phone. He still disapproved of the extra hours she spent with her job, but he seemed pleased she'd made an effort to cut back. Henry promised herself she would make a date with him for the weekend.

They held hands as they stood outside Polly's apartment. As he knocked on the door, Rick smiled warmly at Henry, the March sun no competition for his expression. She thought her own heart would burst with hope; she had missed being with him.

Polly opened the door, a smile lighting her own face when she saw Rick. "Hello! It's good to see you. And Henry! Won't you come in?"

"How've you been, Polly?" Rick said as she shut the door behind them.

"Busy as ever." She grinned, tucking stray blond hair behind her ear. "But pleased with the results. My group is very dedicated to this project."

She gestured at the sofa. "Have a seat. I'll bring out some lemonade."

"I'll help," Rick said, following her to the kitchen.

Henry sank into the overstuffed cotton sofa, amazed at the spotless white material. Polly would probably have kids so well-behaved they'd never even spill a crumb or leave smudges on the glass coffee table.

She glanced around the room. Rick was right. Polly did have a well-decorated apartment. With white cotton-covered chairs to match the sofa, a rattan and glass table and mirror, and hanging ferns, the apartment looked like a tropical paradise. Henry thought guiltily about the one straggly ivy in her living room and resolved to water and feed it more carefully.

Polly emerged from the kitchen, bearing a tray with tall, thick glasses filled with lemonade.

Henry accepted one and took a sip. "Mmm. Delicious. And these glasses are so unusual. Are they imported from Mexico?"

"No." Polly glanced away modestly. "I blew them myself."

Henry nearly choked on her lemonade. "You did?"

"I studied with a glass blower several years ago."

"Isn't that great?" Rick said. "She's such an artist. Wait till she shows you the clothes she's made. And the afghans she and her group have knitted."

"I like to make things," Polly said, blushing. "It's nothing."

"Nothing?" Rick set down his glass on a woven coaster. "It's wonderful! Our church is fortunate you joined when you did. Your group's work is going to put the personal touch to this program."

Henry forced a smile and a murmured agreement. Rick's eyes shone like a kid who'd discovered buried treasure, his admiration for Polly more than evident not only in his words but his expression. Henry's palms grew damp against the heavy glass. She set her lemonade down on a coaster identical to Rick's. Polly had probably woven those, too.

"Shall we get down to business?" Henry said abruptly, flipping open her leather notebook.

Polly's shy smile fell. "Can't it wait awhile, Hen?" Rick said. "This is a good chance for you to get to know Polly. She's been dying to talk to you."

"Yes, Henry," Polly said quietly. "I feel I know you already. Rick talks about you all the time."

Sure, Henry thought. *He probably tells you how I ruin holiday dinners and scorch pots and pans.*

"I'm sorry, Polly," she said in her most businesslike tone, "but I can't chat today. Maybe another time."

"Oh. S-sure," Polly said, her expression hurt.

Rick glanced quizzically at Henry then settled next to her on the couch and related details of Polly's group. Henry scribbled furious notes.

ॐ

On the way home, neither Rick nor Henry said a word. He pulled up outside her house, and they stared at the warm glow emanating behind the drawn living room curtains. Henry rested her elbow in the van's window, open to the spring breeze.

She felt Rick's palm, warm and soft, on her cheek. "Why do I get the feeling lately that I'm losing you?"

Henry managed a weary smile. "I've had a lot on my mind." She put a hand on the door. "And now the kids no doubt need help with their homework. Thank you for taking me to Polly's. I learned a lot."

"Did you, Henry?" he murmured, sliding closer. His fingers curled behind her neck as his face lowered to hers.

"Y-yes. I—"

Rick brushed his lips against hers, silencing her words. The trembling in her stomach intensified, and despite her better sense, she wrapped her arms around his neck.

"Rick," she murmured as he bent his head again, this time for a kiss more passionate than the last.

How had she fallen for this man? They were too much alike, she and he, both of them cut for business talk and action. They worked well as a team, but a husband and wife needed to be more than good decision makers. A home had to have not only heart but someone to manage the day-to-day aspects of living. Rick might want to learn to cook for his children, but he would never be Les. And even if she wanted to give up her career, Henry could never equal the love Nancy had put into maintaining a home.

Rick needed someone like Polly, whose hands and heart could fulfill his life's dreams. Whose confidence and energy could help him raise not only his own children but more of their own. Who was all the things an excellent wife should be.

Henry pulled away quickly, averting her face. "I have to go in," she whispered.

Rick smiled patiently. "But, Henry, I—"

"Thank you, again." She blinked as she fumbled with the door handle.

"Good night," he called softly as she scrambled out of the van in blind haste. "I'll call you tomorrow."

Henry forced back a sob, striding up the walk with her head low.

thirteen

The next evening, Henry stood outside the church and stared at the glass doors. She had come to love the building for more than its wood and stonework. It represented a pillar of stability, a framework of fellow believers who had seen her through some rough emotional times.

She sighed, shoulders slumping. No doubt now she would have to find a new church home.

"Henry!"

She turned, managing a bleak smile. Vera Fabbish waddled toward her in a bright pink and turquoise wind suit, material swishing. She panted under the weight of a large cardboard box in her hands.

"You're here awful early for class," she said, huffing up. She stared at the door, then back at Henry. "What's the matter? Did that old coot Graves leave it locked again?"

Ordinarily Henry would have smiled at the woman's pretend anger at her secret beau, but she wasn't in the mood for teasing. "No, Vera. I've been waiting for you."

Vera flashed her a puzzled glance and shifted the box in her arms. "Come inside and we'll talk, then. Can you hold the door open?"

Henry complied. She let Vera pass, then waited, holding the glass door open.

Vera stared back at her. "Come on, Henry. We can talk in the kitchen."

"No, I. . ." Henry's hand gripped the door tighter. "I just wanted to tell you that I won't be coming to class anymore. I couldn't phone; I had to tell you in person. To thank you for all your help."

Vera set the box on the floor with a thud. "You're dropping out of my class? But the session will be over in a few weeks! And the best part is the graduation dinner."

"I. . .I know," Henry said, losing courage under the woman's hard gaze. "But I just don't have the time anymore to come every week, and—"

"It's Rick, isn't it?" Vera put her hands on her hips. "You're backing out because of him. Did you two have a spat?"

Henry's heart constricted, rising to her throat. "No spat," she said softly, then touched the woman's shoulder quickly before releasing her hold on the door and stepping back. "Good-bye, Vera. Thank you."

The door swung shut. Vera gaped through the glass and Henry fled for her car.

৵

Henry stared at the pile of pink telephone message slips on her desk then glanced at the clock. Rick had called every fifteen minutes since eight o'clock, and it was now ten-fifteen. She'd left the answering machine on at her house last night, and each time she'd heard his voice pleading with her to pick up the phone, she thought her heart would break.

The last message he'd left at her office said in no uncertain terms that if she didn't phone him back, he would call Mr. Fitzhugh and demand to speak to her.

Henry sighed, knowing that she was only putting off the inevitable.

"Hello, Rick," she said quietly when he picked up his phone.

"Hello, yourself," he said in a puzzled tone. "What's up, Henry? I missed you last night, and Vera said something about your not coming to any more classes."

"That's right," she said softly. "I don't have the time anymore. You know how busy I've been."

Silence. "Henry, you're not sick, are you? When Nancy first found out she had cancer, she wouldn't tell me for weeks. But I could tell something was wrong from the way she—"

"I. . .I'm fine."

Rick's sigh was audible. "Thank God."

Silence again. "I need to get back to work," Henry finally said.

"Good. Because you're getting off by six o'clock tonight, and I'm taking you for a drive."

"I don't have time to—"

"I want to show you a project I'm working on just outside of town," he said. "It won't take long, I promise. Bring some work home to do later, but say you'll go with me. I'll treat you to dinner and have you home by eight o'clock."

"Well. . ."

"If you don't say yes, I'll call Mr. Fitzhugh!"

"All right."

"Good!" Rick sounded pleased with himself. "I'll pick you up outside your building to save time, then drive you back to your car when we're through. And Henry?"

Her heart quickened. "Yes?"

"I love you."

"I. . .I have to go, Rick. I'll see you tonight."

She hung up before he could reply, then turned back to the mountain of folders.

❧

Henry gazed out the van's window as they exited the westbound freeway. The office complexes and mini-malls lining the transportation artery of Houston receded to quiet neighborhoods with sidewalks, parks, and play-grounds. Suburbia.

"I thought you only designed office buildings," she said, frowning.

"Not always," he said cheerfully, turning right at a stop sign. He waved at a young girl lugging a box of fund-raising candy.

"Then what—"

"Here we are," he announced, pulling the van to a stop at the end of an undeveloped cul-de-sac.

Henry stared out the window at a large concrete slab with various pipes sticking up like candles on a mutant birthday cake. The heavily wooded area showed signs of recent clearing to make room for the foundation.

"Come on." Rick smiled. "I can't wait to show you."

He was at her side of the van to help her out before she could touch the door handle. Whatever this project was, it certainly meant a lot to him.

Rick encircled her waist with his arm as they plodded the bare earth. The foundation seemed to grow larger as they approached, and Henry's curiosity piqued even more.

"Well?" Rick asked proudly as they stood in front of

the barren cement. "What do you think?"

"I. . ." She turned to him, eyebrows drawn together. "What is it? It's so big. Is it a convenience store?"

He gave her a tender look. "Look here," he said softly, gesturing down. "But watch out. It's still wet. The crew just poured it today."

Henry stared down at the concrete. There at the edge, etched in cement was a large heart. Inside was the inscription R. M. + H. S.

Rick reached in his pocket and pulled out a small, square box. Opening the lid, he held it toward her. A large diamond surrounded by sparkling sapphires nestled in the black velvet.

"For you, Henry," he murmured. "I want to marry you. I want you to be my wife."

Stunned, she gestured at the foundation. "The house . . .You're building it. . .for us?"

He nodded, smiling. "Seven bedrooms, Henry. Plus a study for you and a study for me. We'll all have plenty of room." His voice dropped to an excited murmur. "And God willing, more children to fill it as the older ones move away."

He drew her into his arms, apparently not noticing her shock or the shudder that ran through her. Nuzzling his chin against her hair, he pressed her face against his shoulder. "I love you so much. You've made me so happy. We'll have a wonderful life together, and—"

"No," she mumbled against his shirt. She raised her hands to his chest, blindly pushing herself away.

Rick grasped her arms gently, giving her a blank stare. "No?"

Henry shook her head. "I can't. You're such a wonderful man. . ."

His jaw tightened, and he dropped his arms. "But you won't marry me."

Unable to speak for her clogged throat, she shook her head again. She wrapped her arms around herself, stifling a sob that welled inside her stomach.

Rick snapped the box shut and jammed it back into his pocket. He turned away in frustration, running his fingers through his hair. He stared at the grove of oaks lining the property then spun back around.

"Why? Is it your precious job? Are you afraid I'll encroach upon your work time even more?"

A vision of a shy, blond woman ran through Henry's imagination: Polly baking bread for Rick. . .stitching him flannel shirts. . .decorating the new house. . . sewing her own baby clothes. She was the one for him.

"Yes, Rick," she murmured. "You've never understood how much my job means to me."

"I've tried! Isn't there room in your heart for me and your work?"

She closed her eyes so she wouldn't cry. "P-please take me back to my car. It's late."

She heard him exhale loudly. "It *is* late," he muttered. "Too late."

The van's atmosphere during the drive back to town was iron silence. Henry thought she would choke from the heavy, oppressive sorrow hanging between them like a weighted chain. She hadn't been so unhappy since the day the policeman showed up at the bank to tell her Les had died.

Les. She'd loved him for as long as she could remember, a cherished memory like crystal packed in cotton. Then Rick had shown her how to love again, how to look beyond the daily grind to the promise of tomorrow.

But she'd crossed that nebulous horizon and found tomorrow lacking. Would a promotion—even if she got it—make up for losing Rick?

At least he would have Polly. As he should.

"What floor is your car on?" Rick said tersely as he pulled into the dark parking garage.

She told him, and they ascended the ramps. At last she spied her car at the end of the row, lonely and deserted. Rick pulled up alongside, then put the van in park. Henry noticed he didn't jump out as usual to open her door. Her breathing quickened, and she sought for the right words.

"I guess this is it," he said before she could speak.

She nodded stupidly, reaching for the door handle.

He laid a hand on her arm. Her heart pounded faster, and her eyes met his for the briefest of moments.

He dropped his gaze as though scorched. "Have a good life," he mumbled, releasing her arm.

"You, too," she whispered, then fled from the van.

Rick waited until she was safely in her car, then pulled away as soon as her car's engine turned over. His van disappeared down the ramp.

Henry's gaze followed the fading red glow of his taillights, and she leaned her forehead against the steering wheel and cried.

fourteen

Henry fiddled with the handle of her teacup and glanced around the luxurious home of Mildred Smithwick. She smiled ruefully at the mantel portrait of Mildred and her late husband.

Mildred leaned forward from her place on the velvet settee. She frowned, following the direction of Henry's gaze. "Something wrong with the picture?"

Startled, Henry jerked back to reality. "What? Oh, no, Mildred! It's lovely. I was just thinking how happy the two of you must have been. How long were you married?"

Mildred carefully balanced her china cup and saucer on her knee. "Sixty-three years," she said with pride. She gazed at the portrait with affection. "Robert always referred to me as his child bride. I felt mighty old at the time, but I was only a girl." She giggled. "Hardly had a lick of sense, either. I hadn't been anywhere but the farthest edge of my daddy's farm in Central Texas."

Henry smiled. "You and your husband must have loved each other very much."

"Oh, my, yes. Robert was a wonderful man. But at the end, he was so sick. It was a blessing to give him back to the Lord."

Henry took a slow sip of lukewarm tea. "It was difficult at first for me to admit my husband had died. I didn't have any warning."

"How did he die?"

"In a car accident. He's been dead over a year now."

Mildred laid a soft, wrinkled hand on Henry's knee. "Is that why you're acting like you feel poorly? When you first came over this afternoon, I thought maybe you were sick. But you've got the look of someone who's pining for a lost loved one."

"In a way, I am." She turned from Mildred's knowing eyes, finding it easier to speak to the wall. "A few months ago I met a man at church. . .someone I thought was very special. He. . .well, he thought I was special, too."

"But he broke off with you?"

"No, he asked me to marry him, and I refused."

Mildred's face fell. "But if you cared for him, why?"

"We're just not right for each other. We're too much alike."

Mildred pursed her lips. "Pardon me for saying so, dear, but that's the feeblest excuse I've ever heard for turning down a marriage proposal!"

Henry felt her face flame. "We're both too involved with our careers," she said. "And since we would have six children between us—not to mention any future children—someone needs to stay home to—"

"Wait a minute!"

Henry blinked. "I beg your pardon?"

Mildred smiled sweetly. "I said, 'wait a minute,' young lady. In this age of day care and maids, are you trying to tell me you turned down a marriage proposal because neither one of you wants to defrost the refrigerator?"

"Well, it's not quite like—"

"And you can't tell me, Henrietta Steelman, that you truly like your job."

Henry frowned. *Did* she like her job? Or had she been so busy she hadn't realized the work no longer satisfied her?

"Close your mouth, dear," Mildred said demurely over the rim of her teacup. "It's not becoming."

Henry clamped her lips together, her face burning. "I need my job," she said with quiet determination. "I have children to feed."

"Even if you married this man you're so obviously in love with?" Mildred murmured nonchalantly into her tea.

"Yes! I would go crazy trying to take care of a house. I like to handle business deals, not mops!"

Mildred set her teacup and saucer on the low mahogany table. "Running a home *is* a business," she said. "Look at the wife in Proverbs 31. She took care of her household. . .including the servants. Obviously she didn't do everything by herself. And didn't she consider a field and buy it? She must have been a shrewd businesswoman. The Bible says she brought honor to her husband's name."

Henry considered Mildred's words. Somehow those images had never stood out before, only the wife's duties she herself had trouble with.

"God didn't intend us to be constantly on our hands and knees cleaning," Mildred went on. "He gave us brains, too, to use for our family's benefit. A great deal of intelligence goes into caring for a home, for a family.

It's not all car pools and cooking. It's participating in PTAs. . .just like boardrooms. Planning children's parties. . .just like business agendas. Delegating responsibilities to the children. . .just like employees."

She leaned forward. "But whether we work outside the home or not, we are to love our children and spouses while we can. Having already lost your husband, surely you can see that."

"But—"

"And what about working at home? If you feel you can't last a day without a desk and a daily planner, why don't you find some work you can do out of your house?"

Her face brightened. "In fact, I need someone to run the foundation you've convinced me to start. I plan to do a lot of traveling and charity work, so I don't have the time to consider requests from various agencies who could use my money. I'd also like to start my own charity and give money to needy students or causes. Like your church's Bread and Fish program."

Henry gripped her saucer so tightly she thought the china might snap between her hands. "This is all so sudden, Mildred. I can't just leave my job."

"Why not? It might give you the new perspective you need."

"New perspective? Who says that's what I need?"

"I do! Anybody who would refuse a marriage proposal from a man she's obviously in love with had certainly better get her priorities straight."

Henry set aside her teacup and dragged her briefcase from the floor to her lap. "If you're going to continue to harp on my personal life, it's time we got down to business and settled your own affairs."

"Fine, dear," Mildred said. "I guess you don't need to hear the ramblings of an old lady, after all."

She flashed a sanguine smile and primly pulled the skirt of her fashionable suit over her knees as she edged closer to Henry.

જ

That night Henry made a special point to get home in time to fix dinner for Cindy and Brian. Using the recipe Vera had given the class several months ago, Henry baked a poppy seed, chicken casserole and scalloped potatoes and fixed a Caesar salad. But by the time she set the perfectly cooked meal on the table, she didn't have the heart to eat.

Cindy and Brian dug in with gusto, even asking for second helpings before Henry had scarcely tasted her own food. She dug trenches in her potatoes and picked at the succulent skin of the chicken, her mind miles away from the table.

Rick.

How was he doing? She'd thought maybe he'd phone—she'd begun to hope he *would* phone—but he was as silent as though they'd never met.

Once or twice she'd even attended the second church service—his usual time—but she hadn't caught so much as a glimpse of him. She even sat in the balcony, hoping for just a look. He either wasn't attending church or was staying well-hidden.

"Didn't you hear me, Mom?" Brian nudged her elbow.

Startled, Henry sat up straight. Two pairs of eyes

stared at her, and she flashed a sheepish grin. "I'm sorry, Brian. . .Cindy. What were you saying?"

Brian's face fell. "I said that I think dinner is a lot more fun with the three of us."

Henry's smile widened. "It sure is. If it takes going in to work at six o'clock, I'll do it. I've missed a lot of dinners with you two, and I'm going to try to make it up from now on."

"What about the cooking class, Mom?" Cindy asked timidly. She exchanged a quick glance with her brother, who quickly dropped his gaze to his lap. "What about Mr. Montgomery?"

Henry set her mouth in a firm line. "The cooking class is over, as far as I'm concerned. And I won't be seeing Rick anymore."

"You won't?" Brian looked surprised. His expression turned serious, a little too quickly, Henry thought. "Oh, Mom," he said, "that's a shame."

"Yeah." Cindy lowered her gaze. "I liked Rachel and Clara," she mumbled.

Henry picked up her fork with renewed purpose, forcing a bright tone. "Well, we won't be seeing them anymore, so it'll just be the three of us. Mrs. Maldonado won't be coming back either, so we'll just have to make do again until I can see about getting another maid."

"I can fold clothes," Cindy said quickly.

"After I wash them," Brian added.

Henry smiled at her children, resisting the urge to rumple their hair the way she'd done when they were smaller. Their eagerness was the best encouragement she'd had lately. Surely it wouldn't be long before she could put her other troubles behind her, as well.

Later, as they settled in to play a spirited game of Parcheesi, more than once she found her mind wandering back to Rick or back to the mountain of work at the office. The children behaved better than they had in a long while. It almost seemed they were trying to make up for her recent heartache.

❧

Henry stared at her desk telephone, mesmerized, subconsciously willing it to ring. Only a few minutes remained until her daily meeting with Mr. Fitzhugh. Shaking her head with impatience, she settled down to the work laid out in front of her.

Paperwork. Meetings to schedule with customers, meetings to attend with her workers, and meetings to endure with Mr. Fitzhugh. A never-ending cycle.

Oh God, Father, what am I supposed to do?

The phone jangled. Quicker than usual, she picked up the receiver. "Henry Steelman," she said breathlessly, heart fluttering against her ribs.

"Henry. It's Mary Montgomery."

Henry automatically straightened. "How are you, Mary?"

"I'm fine." She paused. "How are you?"

"I'm fine, too."

Henry paused, swiveling her chair around until she stared at the calendar on her wall. "Mary, this is probably as uncomfortable for me as it for you, but. . ."

"You want to know how Rick is?"

"Well. . .Yes." There. She'd admitted it to herself as well as someone else.

"I've seen him in better shape. Graham brought the kids over to my house last night just to get away from him. They said he's been quite grumpy lately."

Henry forced a dry laugh. "I hope he's not taking it out on them."

"He's taking his heartbreak out on everyone," Mary said in clipped tones. "But that's not why I called, Henry. I just wanted to make sure *you* were all right."

Henry's eyebrows drew together. "I'm fine. Work keeps me busy, and the kids—"

"Oh, I'm terrible at lying," Mary broke in. She sighed. "I know it's not my place to butt in, but I wanted you to know just how upset Rick is that you refused to marry him."

Henry gripped the phone. "What's wrong, Mary?"

The older woman sighed again. "He's seeing Polly Faradon."

fifteen

"Polly?" Henry's voice came out in a squeak. She cleared her throat. "That's good news. Rick and Polly seem to like one another very much. Polly's a wonderful woman." Her voice dropped to a whisper and she squeezed her eyes shut. "And Rick's a wonderful man."

My son's a *foolish* man. He obviously did something to upset you. I don't know why—"

A sharp rap sounded at the glass next to Henry's closed door. Startled, she glanced up to see Mr. Fitzhugh glowering through the window as though she were Bob Cratchit and he, Ebenezer Scrooge. She held up a finger in Mr. Fitzhugh's direction to indicate the momentary conclusion of her phone call.

"Mary, I have to go," she said. "Can I call you another—"

"I *did* call you with a real reason; not to throw Polly Faradon in your face. Vera Fabbish asked me to call you. There's a Bread and Fish meeting on Thursday night and she needs you to attend."

"I don't think that would be appropriate, under the circumstances," Henry said. "In fact, I've considered resigning—"

The rap at the window sounded again. This time Mr. Fitzhugh pointed at his watch and glared.

Desperate, Henry leaned closer to the phone receiver,

anxious to conclude the conversation. "What time on Thursday?"

"Seven-thirty. Fellowship Hall. And Henry?"

She cast a quick glance at her angry boss. "Yes?"

"Please be there. Don't let Rick keep you away."

"I wouldn't dream of it," Henry said automatically. "Thank you for calling."

She hung up before she could hear Mary's response and leapt from her chair. Mr. Fitzhugh burst through her door, his face and neck still flushed above his stiff white collar and navy blue jacket.

"May I remind you that—"

"I'm sorry, Mr. Fitzhugh. I finished the call as quickly as I could."

"Hmmph. It was a *personal* call, too!" he huffed, folding his arms in front of his chest.

Henry balled her hands into fists. He had eavesdropped!

She drew a calming breath. "I said I was sorry. The call was about a committee that I'm on at church, and—"

Mr. Fitzhugh made a bored face. "I'm only interested in your work for First Houston. Not your personal life."

"No, you're not, are you?" Henry said. A catch lodged in her throat, and she clutched the desk with one hand for support. "You've never cared anything about me, Louise, or anyone else in this office. Do you even know I'm a widow?"

"Well, I—"

"Or that I have two beautiful children growing up faster than the work you throw my way? You know I'll do it just because I want to make vice president. I've risked precious time with my family by trying to please you."

Henry advanced a step and Mr. Fitzhugh backed against the doorjamb. The color drained from his face. Henry's head told her she should back down and apologize, but her heart overruled. She'd lost Rick, but she wouldn't lose her children, too.

She drew a deep breath. "I quit."

Clayton Fitzhugh smirked. "You'll never have a chance at another vice presidency in Houston. I personally guarantee it."

His words drove straight to her heart, seizing her with the impulse to tremble. Instead, she held herself erect and still, sending up a quiet prayer for strength. Instantly she was flooded with the sensation of rightness. She hadn't felt such reassurance for a long time, probably because she'd been ignoring God, too.

"It doesn't matter if I ever work in a bank again," she said quietly. "That may not be where God wants me, after all."

He laughed. "You'll wind up taking the first low-paying job that becomes available."

"I'll work wherever I'm called, but I know it won't be at the expense of my family."

Henry reached in the trash can for an empty box. Without a word, she loaded it with her coffee mug and pictures of Les and the kids. Mr. Fitzhugh watched with a look of silent disbelief. Henry hooked her purse strap over her shoulder and lifted the box.

Chin high, she made her way to the door, then paused

and turned. "I'm sorry I couldn't be the automaton you wanted, but I'm more sorry you don't understand the importance of love and family. I hope it doesn't take you much longer than it already took me."

She headed for the elevator.

Once in her car, she drove from the garage's stifling darkness into the warm glow of the spring morning. Driving in midday downtown traffic seemed dreamlike. Normally if she were on Texas Street, she'd be on foot, delivering a sensitive document or searching for a quick, greasy lunch.

Only when she left the stair-stepped Houston skyline behind and hit the Loop did she realize she clutched the steering wheel like a novice driver. Laughing, she let out a long breath and eased her posture and grip.

"Face it, Henrietta, you're a free woman. You may not be eating for much longer, but you've finally left the clutches of that man. Mildred was right. You really *didn't* like that job. Now you'll have much more time to be the mom to Brian and Cindy you need to be."

Her conscience twinged. Before, it had always been a matter of not being able to cook for her kids; now it was an issue of not even having the money to feed them.

She shook off her fear with resolution. "Okay, God, I'm going to trust in You and not lean on my own understanding. You lead the way and I'll follow."

She pulled into her driveway and braked, staring at the brick structure she called home. Funny how different the house looked in the middle of a weekday. It looked much more expensive. Would God truly provide food, mortgage, and all the other necessities of life?

Henry pressed the remote and smiled as the heavy

garage door slowly raised. "Just for today, I really am going to consider the lilies of the field," she said, grinning. "It feels good to be free."

✦

Cindy and Brian gaped, their backpacks sagging from their hands as they stood outside the bathroom. "Mom?"

Henry raised up from where she bent over the tub and waved a soapy hand in greeting. "Hi, kids! How was school? Give me two hours to finish both bathrooms and vacuum, then I'm taking you out to celebrate. You pick the place."

"Celebrate what?" Brian said warily.

Henry winked. "I think I'll save that for dinner. Now off with you, and finish your homework so we can take our time tonight."

Two hours later they pulled out of the driveway, the children still puzzled and Henry still cheerful. "Where do you want to eat?"

Brian glanced at Cindy, then shrugged. "Pizza?"

"Pizza it is!"

When they pulled up to the pizza parlor, her enthusiasm fizzled into uncertainty. For the second time that day she remembered Rick. The last time she'd been here was Christmas Eve.

"Come on, Mom, what's the surprise?" Cindy tugged at Henry's sleeve.

"Let's order first, then I'll tell you," she said as she slid across the booth's vinyl upholstery.

While Cindy and Brian selected music for the jukebox, Henry fingered a paper place mat. What would Rick have thought of her quitting? He'd thought she worked too much, but would he think her irresponsible for abandoning a steady income?

Brian and Cindy took their seats. "We ordered at the counter, so tell us what's going on."

Henry smiled crookedly. "I quit my job."

"You *what?*"

"I quit. Mr. Fitzhugh was absolutely impossible, and I realized I was tired of not spending time with you. I'm sorry I've ignored you both."

Cindy looked guiltily at Brian, then back at Henry. "We thought maybe you'd agreed to marry Mr. Montgomery," she said softly.

Henry felt an ache in her heart, not only for herself but for the hurt expression on her daughter's face. That was peculiar; she'd thought Cindy and Brian didn't like Rick.

"No, honey. I thought you understood that Mr. Montgomery and I aren't seeing each other anymore."

"Oh," Cindy said in a small voice, lowering her eyes. She slumped her elbows on the table and fixed her gaze on the chrome napkin dispenser.

Brian cleared his throat. "Why aren't you seeing him anymore?"

"We're just not suited for each other, Brian. Mr. Montgomery. . .Rick. . .needs someone more domestic than me."

"You sure looked domestic enough this afternoon," Brian muttered, glancing at Cindy. She raised her eyes and exchanged a guilty stare with her brother before both heads bowed.

Henry frowned. What was wrong with these two?

Cindy glared at Brian. "Well, if you're not going to tell her, I am!"

"Tell me what?"

Brian sighed, dragging his gaze to meet Henry's. "We deliberately messed up that Saturday-night dinner with the Montgomerys."

Henry drew back in surprise, speechless.

"We didn't want you to get married to him!" Cindy piped up, her expression earnest. "But that was before we got to know his kids. And he *has* always been nice to us." She glared at Brian again. "I don't care what you say!"

"He wasn't so bad," Brian conceded, then added, "neither was Graham."

Perplexed, Henry studied her children. "What do you mean you messed up the dinner?"

"We figured if he could see you weren't good around the house, he wouldn't want to marry you," Brian said. "I called Mrs. Maldonado and told her you were sick so she wouldn't clean."

"So *that's* why she didn't show up! But she. . .Brian, you know Mrs. Maldonado doesn't speak English. What Spanish word did you use to tell her I was sick?"

"*En. . .en. . .*" He squeezed his eyes shut in concentration.

"*Encinta?*"

Brian looked relieved. "Yeah, that's it."

Henry suppressed a smile. "That means pregnant! Mrs. Maldonado thought I was pregnant."

"Oh."

" 'Oh' is right." Henry's smile widened. The two little wretches had certainly gone to a lot of trouble. "Did you two also plan that little cookie mess in the kitchen?"

Brian and Cindy nodded.

"And that sudden need to go to Adam's was a ruse to

keep me from cleaning house?"

Brian nodded again, sheepish.

Henry leaned forward on her elbows, trying to keep her voice stern. "That was a very selfish thing you both did. I'm hurt that you wouldn't even tell me how you felt about Rick. Did you think I would marry a man you two didn't like?"

Brian and Cindy glanced at each other. "Well, you weren't exactly always at home," he said. "And we figured if you married him, you'd have even less time for us."

Henry considered his statement in the light of two children who had lost their father the past year and their mother to a busy career. Her heart flooded with compassion, and she said a silent prayer of thanks that her eyes had finally been opened. How foolish she'd been.

She laid a hand on a shoulder of each child. "That's going to change. I have to find another job to support us, but I promise I'll never let it come between me and the two of you again." She paused. "And as for you two trying to keep Rick away, I forgive you for that."

Cindy and Brian glanced at each other, then turned relieved expressions to their mother.

"Thanks," Brian said. "I'm sorry we didn't try to talk to you, Mom. And I'm sorry for the stupid stunts we pulled."

"Yeah," Cindy echoed, "me, too."

"Then it's forgotten." Henry leaned back, making way for the server to set down their pizzas. "Come on, guys, dig in!"

sixteen

Henry combed her hair with her fingers and drew a steadying breath as she entered the church building. Light from the lengthening spring evening filtered into the empty corridor, and a flickering fluorescent bulb lit the way to the fellowship hall.

Before she could take more than five steps, the door opened behind her. With a knowing sense of dread, she paused. A lively conversation between a deep voice and a higher-pitched female one abruptly halted, and two sets of footsteps hushed against the carpet. The weighted door banged shut against the frame.

"Hello, Henry," Rick said.

Henry pasted a smile on her face. "Hi, Rick. Polly." Hopefully her voice sounded steadier to their ears than her own.

Polly's normally serene face looked mortified. "H-hello, Henry. How are you?"

"Fine, thank you." She bobbed her head, the fixed smile feeling as solid as one of Vera's sponge cakes.

Polly drew a short breath. "I'm glad we're having this meeting tonight. I. . .I mean, so that we can talk about the program." She glanced at Rick as though for support. He kept his eyes fixed somewhere beyond Henry, who could see his shoulders raise once as though he'd drawn a long breath.

Polly flushed. "Excuse me, but I have to go to the ladies' room. I'll meet you in the hall." Her low-heeled pumps swished against the worn carpet as she scurried in the opposite direction.

Rick and Henry stared at one another for a long, awkward moment. She desperately tried to think of something to say, but drew a blank.

Face expressionless, Rick took the initiative. "How have you been?"

"Fine." Her insides turned to jelly. "And you?"

"The same." He paused. "How's your job?"

Henry's heart leapt to her throat. If she told him, maybe he would—

"It's fine, too," she heard herself say calmly.

Silence. Henry straightened. "I guess we'd better go in."

Rick stared as though searching her eyes. He finally broke the gaze and glanced down the hall. "You go ahead. I'll wait for Polly."

Henry cleared her throat. "I'm anxious to hear what you and Polly have done."

He turned his gaze back to her.

"I mean about the food program."

She wanted to run down the hall—or straight out the building—but she forced a steady gait down the hall. Why had she been so shocked to see Rick and Polly together? Mary Montgomery had warned her.

Vera Fabbish met her in the doorway of the crowded room. "Hello, dear," she said above the hushed conversations. "You haven't returned my calls about the program lately. I was beginning to think you'd dropped off the face of the earth."

"I'm sorry," Henry said, feeling genuine regret. "To be honest, I thought about resigning and I didn't want to face you. I didn't want you to be disappointed."

"Disappointed? In you?" Vera's dangling silver coin earrings jangled against her neck as she laughed. "Nonsense. I didn't take any offense about your dropping out of my class, if that's what you're thinking. And if you're truly too busy to handle the food program, I'd understand."

Henry caught a choking whiff of gardenia perfume as Vera leaned closer. "But if you dropped out of my class or this program because of a certain young man," Vera whispered, "why, you're right. I *would* be disappointed. You're too smart to let a little heartache stop you."

Henry tore her gaze from the older woman's knowing eyes. "Thanks for the vote of confidence," she muttered.

Vera straightened. Her coral-colored lips parted and curled upward. "Then you'll be at my graduation dinner for the cooking class!"

Henry glanced nervously at the door just as Rick and Polly entered. "Well, I. . ."

Vera planted her fists against green spandex hips. "Two weeks from Saturday here in this hall."

Henry cut her eyes at Rick and Polly. They moved through the crowd, chatting comfortably. Polly would probably show up on Rick's arm for the graduation dinner, as well.

She swallowed hard, then squared her shoulders. She might have lingering feelings for Rick, but just to prove to him, Polly, and Vera—everyone, if not herself—

she'd go to the dinner and have a good time. Vera Fabbish *had* taught her how to cook, after all.

She took Vera's hand. "I'll be there. Should I bring something?"

Vera's eyes gleamed. "Just yourself." She turned away to speak to Pastor Reynolds, then tilted her head with a final aside to Henry. "And wear something nice. It's a formal dinner."

Henry shrugged, then took her place at the podium. She cupped her hands around her mouth to be heard over the room's din. "Attention! We're ready to start."

All eyes turned forward and everyone found a seat. She waited until they had settled comfortably on the metal folding chairs, then smiled warmly. She noticed out of her peripheral vision that Rick and Polly were in seats up front, on her right.

"Thank you for coming and for your hard work," she said. "I'd like to give a report on my committee, then we'll hear from Polly Faradon's."

She paused. "But first let's open with a prayer." She bowed her head, squeezing her eyes shut to force her attention on God instead of the man sitting down front.

"Father, thank You for the love You have given us and that we can return that love through the corporate body of this church. Bless the fruit of our hands, Lord, and use it as You see fit. Amen."

"Amen," the crowd murmured.

Henry raised her head, inadvertently catching Rick's gaze. For a moment their eyes held. The room receded, and Henry could see—*knew*—he still loved her. She wanted to push the podium aside and fling herself in his arms to babble her regret and confess her own love for him.

Polly leaned over to whisper something in Rick's ear. Henry blinked, then glanced out over the crowd. She cleared her throat and clasped her hands behind her back for support. She dug her fingers into her wrists as she watched Polly and Rick share whatever information they had between them.

"I've been in contact with a fairly wealthy widow interested in supporting our organization," Henry said. "She's also asked me to speak to several of her friends. If they're interested, we'll raise even more money. I've also spoken with the heads of several homeless shelters, runaway centers, and other churches to help get out the word about our services."

A murmur of approval rippled through the crowd. Henry forced herself not to look at Rick. He would probably be displeased with her businesslike approach to the situation. She didn't have a tangible product to show for her efforts, only good intentions and promises.

"That's all I have," she said, deflated. "Polly, I turn the floor over to you."

"Thank you, Henry." Polly rose, then made her way to the podium. She, too, clasped her hands behind her back and timidly told of her group's work of potential menus and clothing sewn. Henry only half-heartedly listened. She'd already seen Polly's handiwork.

When the meeting was over, Henry made her escape as quickly as possible. As she inserted her key in the car door, she heard hurried footsteps. Polly and Rick stood behind her.

"I didn't get a chance to tell you what a great job you've done," Polly said breathlessly. "I don't know how you manage to speak so well or to find the courage to ask people for money."

Henry shrugged. "Thanks, Polly. It's nothing."

"No, it was wonderful, Henry," Rick said. He started to touch her shoulder, then drew his hand back. "That was good work. You have a real knack."

Henry turned the key before tears formed in her eyes. "I'll see you at the next meeting," she murmured, then whipped open the car door. She saw Rick and Polly walk toward his minivan, and she gunned the engine.

❧

"What's the matter with Mom?" Cindy whispered as she and Brian rinsed dinner dishes.

He glanced at the living room, where Henry read the paper. "You mean, why has she been reading the same page for thirty minutes?" he whispered back.

Cindy nodded. "Do you think she misses Mr. Montgomery?"

"I know she does." Brian grimaced. "She hasn't moped around the house this much since Dad died."

Cindy scraped a plate under the running water then handed it to her brother. "Maybe we could call him."

"No way. I ran into Graham Montgomery, and he said his dad's been miserable, too."

Brian wiped his hands on a kitchen towel, contemplating. He cast another glance at the living room, then smiled. "You keep an eye on Mom. I'm going to make a phone call."

Cindy sighed with exasperation. "Haven't you had

enough scheming?"

"We got her into this mess; and it's up to us to get her out. Just keep her in that room, Cinder-face. I'm going to check with someone who's older and sneakier."

"Who's that?"

Brian grinned. "Graham Montgomery."

❧

"Henrietta!" Mildred Smithwick said over the phone. "How lovely to hear from you."

Henry grinned. Why had it taken her so long to accept the gift that had been dropped in front of her? "This isn't strictly a social call. I wanted to know if that job offer you made me a while back is still good."

"You mean the foundation directorship? Why, yes! Are you interested?"

"Only on condition that I can work out of my home. I'd be glad to attend lunches and appointments, but I'd like to do the paperwork out of my house. I can get my own computer and fax and modem and—"

"Slow down!" Mildred laughed. "I didn't realize running a business these days took so many modern conveniences!"

"It does." Henry smiled. "One other thing, though, and for this I'd be willing to take a pay cut."

"What's that, dear?"

"I'll need a secretary. I'm a terrible typist."

"Do you have anyone in mind?"

"I most certainly do. My ex-secretary from the office. The last time I talked to her, she was still unemployed. She has a little boy and would be glad to work at home, too. We can probably exchange information through our computers without ever leaving the house."

Mildred's tone turned serious. "Tell me your salary at First Houston."

Henry named a figure and felt her stomach twist when Mildred didn't immediately respond. "That's more money than I can spend, Henrietta," she finally murmured. "Especially with a secretary, too."

"I thought so." Henry paused. "Can you afford two-thirds? Between me and the secretary?"

Mildred considered. "I think the foundation can survive that." She paused. "If you can."

Henry smiled at the receiver. "Believe me, it'll be worth it. And I know Louise will think so, too."

"Good. Then invite the young lady over to my house tomorrow, and we'll discuss the details. Meanwhile, we'll write the foundation's first check to the Bread and Fish program."

"You're a dream come true, Mildred."

The older woman chuckled. "I was just about to say the same for you, Henrietta Steelman."

seventeen

Hair in curlers and clad in her terry-cloth bathrobe, Henry deliberated in front of her closet.

"Wear the black dress, Mom," Cindy urged. "The one you wore on New Year's Eve."

"Not that one." Henry rifled through the hangered clothes. "Vera said the dinner was formal, but I couldn't."

"Why not?"

"You're too young to understand," Henry muttered.

"It's your prettiest dress!"

"And it reminds me of a marvelous night, Cindy. Besides, Rick's already seen me in it. A lady tries never to wear the same dress twice in front of a man."

"I thought you said you weren't seeing him anymore. Do you care whether he notices?"

Henry paused with her hand at the shoulder of a severe gray suit jacket. *Was* she hoping to capture Rick's attention?

"Nonsense!" she said, as much to herself as Cindy.

"Then you'll wear it?"

Face hidden, Cindy kneeled to study the closet's line of shoes. If Henry didn't know better, she'd say her daughter was smiling.

Henry sighed. She didn't have much of a choice. "I'll wear the dress." She peeled back the cleaner's plastic, rejoicing that the dress was clean.

She frowned. That was funny. She thought she'd hung it back in the closet right after wearing it New Year's Eve. Getting clothes to the cleaners had always been a problem.

Henry scooped up the plastic from where she'd tossed it on the floor. Maybe a dated bill would jog her memory.

"I think the shoes with the little black straps would look nice," Cindy said, holding up a preferred pair.

Henry ran the plastic wrap through her hands.

"Looking for something, Mom?" Cindy leaned against the closet door.

"The cleaning bill. I don't remember taking this dress in."

Cindy shrugged. "You took it in back in February, I think."

"I don't remember." Henry frowned. "And as much as this dress meant. . ."

She trailed off, exasperated. What difference did it make? The dress was clean. The last few months had been so hectic, it was a wonder she even knew where her closet was.

"Here." Cindy shoved the shoes in her hands. "Get dressed then come out and show me. Then I'll watch you put on your makeup."

Henry smiled, smoothing the dress between her hands. "You can help me brush out my hair, if you want, too."

Cindy beamed at the offer to help make her mother glamorous.

By the time Henry was ready to leave the house,

every curl and every flake of powder had come under the scrutiny of Cindy's critical eyes. Her daughter talked her into emulating a celebrity hairstyle they'd seen.

"The magazine was right. It's definitely sophisticated and alluring." Cindy stepped back from arranging the last soft curl. "Guaranteed to turn heads."

Henry laughed, twisting her neck from side to side to see the upswept style's full effect. "I don't care about turning heads. I just don't want people to remember how my cooking used to turn stomachs."

Brian slouched against the door frame. "You don't do that anymore, Mom. You've gotten a lot better."

"I've learned more than how to cook," she said. "Mostly that I'm lucky to be able to stay at home now. A lot of moms need jobs, inside or outside their homes. What matters most, though, is that family comes first."

Brian ducked his head. "Aw, Mom. Did you have to get so mushy?"

Cindy glanced at her brother, then back to Henry. "You'd better get going, or you'll be late."

Henry smiled. "Thanks for all the help, Peaches. I don't know why you made such a fuss over me. It's just a silly dinner. But I feel better all dressed up."

Cindy led her by the arm toward the garage. "You look great. Have fun."

"Yeah," Brian mumbled, unsuccessfully trying to look disinterested. "Have a good time."

The careful attention to her fashion lifted Henry's spirits considerably, and by the time she arrived at the church, she was singing along with the radio.

She glanced around as she shut the car door. That was odd. There were only two other cars in the lot—Rick's and Vera's. She looked down at her wrist then remembered she hadn't worn a watch. Was she early?

The corridor was silent and eerie as she made her way to the fellowship hall. She clutched her handbag, eyeing her own shadow with skepticism.

"Behave yourself, Henrietta," she muttered. "There's nothing unusual about. . ."

The fellowship hall was dark and empty.

Henry didn't even bother to flip the light switch. Obviously no dinner was scheduled to take place here tonight. She must have gotten her dates mixed up.

Disappointed, she slunk back down the hall. Just as she put her hand on the glass door, she heard voices in the kitchen. Curious, she followed the noise, wondering what Vera and Rick were up to.

As she drew closer, she could hear the confusion in Rick's voice. ". . .but Graham said you were interested in buying the ring."

Henry leaned against the door frame. She recognized the small velvet box he held out to Vera, who suddenly turned.

"Henry!" She bustled to the doorway. "I'm so glad you could make it. Come in, come in."

The large, hot pink bow at the back of Vera's head bounced as the woman nodded vigorously. She wore an equally loud pink chiffon dress, covered with a white ruffled apron. Henry smiled. Any other cook would have at least a minute stain on an apron that white. Not Vera Fabbish.

Rick tucked the box into his jacket pocket. Henry

recognized the suit as the same one he'd worn on New Year's Eve. Out of all the well-tailored suits she'd seen him wear, why did he have to wear this one tonight?

Rick's expression was puzzled. "Hello, Henry. What are you doing here?"

She took a step forward, closer to the steel counter where he stood. "Even though I didn't finish the class, Vera invited me."

She glanced around. "By the way, where is the rest of the class?"

Rick chuckled, folding his arms across his chest. "I was beginning to wonder that myself."

Click.

They whirled around to the door. It had shut firmly, and they heard a key turn.

"What—" Rick stormed forward and turned the knob. It refused to budge.

"Hey!" He pounded on the door. "We're locked in here."

Suspicion mounting, Henry glanced around. "Where's Vera?"

"Why, she's right—" Rick turned. His mouth dropped in shock, then he quickly recovered. He chuckled. "That crafty old woman."

"What?" Henry strode toward him, heels tapping a staccato across the linoleum. Had everyone gone crazy?

Rick raised laughing eyes. "Don't you get it, Henry? She's thrown us together so we'll patch things up."

Henry felt heat rise to her face. "That's ridiculous."

"Is it?" a voice called sweetly through the door. "It's what the two of you want, you ninnies."

"Vera," Rick warned, "enough is enough. Let us out."

They heard a sharp laugh. "Not on your life, mister. Your kids and I went to a lot of trouble to arrange this, so you might as well at least enjoy the meal I prepared for you."

"Our kids?" Henry called. "Were they in on this?"

"It was their idea. It seems they now like the idea of having a new mom or dad."

"Wait till I get my hands on Brian and Cindy," Henry seethed. "If they think I'm going to forgive them for interfering again. . ."

"What do you mean, interfering again?" Rick said.

She sighed, shoulders slumping. "The night we ordered the Chinese food for all the kids. Remember what a fiasco the day had been for me? My kids were behind all that. They wanted you to think I was a lousy housekeeper so you wouldn't want to marry me."

Rick laughed. "I'm afraid their stunt had the wrong effect. I wanted to marry you even more!"

Henry's heart thumped against her chest. "You did?" she whispered.

Rick's eyes shone, warm. "Yes, Henry. You looked completely frazzled, but you accepted it all with grace. I knew that night you would be a wife equal to any challenge life threw us."

Henry felt her heart rise then sink again. She turned away. "Polly would be better for you."

"Polly!"

She nodded, unable to speak.

Rick gripped her arms, and a shudder of pleasure rippled through her at his touch. She tried to pull away in embarrassment, but he held her firmly.

"You think Polly would make a better wife?"

"I thought she was what you wanted. What you needed."

Rick turned her around, raising her chin with a gentle hand until their eyes met. "I could never feel for Polly what I feel for you, Henry," he said softly. "I told you before I thought you were a special woman, and I'll always think that."

Henry felt tears glistening in her eyes. She wanted to look away, but his hazel eyes glowed with sincerity, revealing his hurt.

"I thought you didn't need a businesswoman for a wife," she whispered.

Rick's hands clasped her shoulders, but his eyes never left her face. "I need *you,*" he whispered. "Just as you are. The gifts you have as a businesswoman are just as important as Polly's gift of crafts. We all have different talents, Henry. It's what we do with them that counts."

He dropped his hands and turned away. "But I guess you'd rather spend your time at the office than with a family."

Henry laughed through her tears, joy bubbling her heart. "I quit my job," she said. "I'm going to be the foundation director for the woman who's funding the Bread and Fish program. I'll be working at home so I can spend more time with my family."

"What happened? You loved your job. You wanted to get ahead."

She shook her head. "Not anymore. Mr. Fitzhugh put so many demands on me and treated everyone in the office like robots instead of human beings. I quit not long after you and I stopped seeing each other."

Rick smiled tenderly, touching her face. "And you

refused to marry me because of Polly?"

Henry nodded. "Then when your mother told me you were seeing her. . ."

Rick shook his head. "I took Polly out for dinner one night because she wanted to talk about you. She heard we'd broken up, and she wanted to make sure she wasn't the cause. Leave it to my mother to use that to try to get you to call me."

"But at the last meeting you and Polly were together!"

Rick laughed, his eyes dancing. "She had a flat and asked me at the last minute to pick her up. She doesn't care for me, Henry. At least not like you think. She told me I remind her of her older brother." Rick moved closer, his voice lowering. "Not someone who would ever kiss her. . .not like this, anyway."

He bent his head and gently captured her lips with his. Her head swirled and her heart danced. His arms tightened around her, pressing her closer, and his lips moved to her temple.

"I thought I'd lost you, Henrietta. If I ask you again, what will you say?" he whispered against her ear.

A shiver of pleasure rippled through her. "Try me," she murmured dreamily.

"Will you marry me?" he whispered. "Will you walk beside me, before God, as my beloved in His eyes?"

"Yes," she said softly. Her arms tightened around him in a firm embrace. "I will."

They held each other, motionless, savoring. Henry knew the emotional intensity wouldn't last through every moment of their married life, that they would know sorrow and disagreement as well as joy and peace. But as long as they held each other's honor as securely as they now held each other, as long as they listened to the God who had brought them together, the depth of their love could only increase.

"Hmmph!" On the other side of the door, Vera cleared her throat. "It's about time you two got things worked out. Why don't you give her the ring?"

They laughed. Rick withdrew the velvet box and gently placed the diamond on her finger.

"I'll be adding a gold band to that," he said. "But promise you won't make me wait. We've already been apart too long."

Henry nodded, smiling.

"Let us out now, Vera," Rick called. "We need to break the news to the kids."

"No need. I already phoned them while you two were busy spooning. But I *did* cook you a fine dinner. You'd better eat before it gets cold."

Henry glanced at the empty counter. "Where is it?"

"Start with the oven."

Rick and Henry looked at each other with a shrug, then did as Vera suggested. Rick opened the oven door to reveal a succulent steak. He withdrew the platter and plucked a note sticking out under the sirloin.

"'This meat is for the strength you must have to withstand the times of trouble in life,'" he read aloud. "'Go to the first shelf in the pantry.'"

Henry opened the door and took out a covered dish. She removed the lid to find two steaming, baked potatoes. "'These potatoes represent the sustaining life of your love, a necessary staple of any marriage,'" she read, smiling. 'Go to the top of the refrigerator.'"

Rick pulled down a chafing dish from the refrigerator.

Inside were small, braised onions. "'These are to remind you of the tears you must occasionally shed, of the weeping that comes before joy,'" he read from the note attached to the handle. "'Look in the microwave.'"

Henry opened the microwave door, pulling out a covered casserole dish. Inside was a bed of steaming green beans, laced with several pats of melting butter. "'These signify the tenderness with which you must each always regard the other. Look in the refrigerator.'"

Rick opened the door and pulled out a French silk pie, covered with delicate shavings of chocolate. He gently loosened the note taped to the side of the pan. "'This pie represents the sweetness of words and actions for which you should strive.'"

Henry took the pie pan from his hands and set it beside the other food. She swallowed a lump of emotion. "Vera went to all this trouble. . .the kids went to all the trouble. . .just to get us back together," she said, awed.

Rick turned the piece of paper over, frowning. "What comes after dessert, Henry? It says, 'Look under the sink.'"

"The sink? Ugh!"

Together they bent to open the door. Rick withdrew a small fire extinguisher and turned with a grin. "You want to read the note?"

Henry plucked the note from the nozzle, laughing, then wrapped an arm around Rick.

"'In case Henry cooks.'"

A Letter To Our Readers

Dear Reader:

In order that we might better contribute to your reading enjoyment, we would appreciate your taking a few minutes to respond to the following questions. When completed, please return to the following:

Rebecca Germany, Managing Editor
Heartsong Presents
P.O. Box 719
Uhrichsville, Ohio 44683

1. Did you enjoy reading *The Fruit of Her Hands*?
   ❑ Very much. I would like to see more books
      by this author!
   ❑ Moderately
      I would have enjoyed it more if _____

   _____

2. Are you a member of **Heartsong Presents**? ❑Yes ❑No
   If no, where did you purchase this book?_____

   _____

3. What influenced your decision to purchase this
   book? (Check those that apply.)

   ❑ Cover   ❑ Back cover copy

   ❑ Title   ❑ Friends

   ❑ Publicity   ❑ Other_____

4. How would you rate, on a scale from 1 (poor) to 5
   (superior), the cover design? _____

5. On a scale from 1 (poor) to 10 (superior), please rate the following elements.

___Heroine   ___Plot

___Hero   ___Inspirational theme

___Setting   ___Secondary characters

6. What settings would you like to see covered in **Heartsong Presents** books?_____

_____

_____

7. What are some inspirational themes you would like to see treated in future books?_____

_____

_____

8. Would you be interested in reading other **Heartsong Presents** titles? ❑ Yes   ❑ No

9. Please check your age range:
   ❑ Under 18   ❑ 18-24   ❑ 25-34
   ❑ 35-45   ❑ 46-55   ❑ Over 55

10. How many hours per week do you read? _____

Name _____

Occupation_____

Address_____

City_____ State_____ Zip_____

Cook "Inn" Style

with *The Christian Bed & Breakfast Cookbook*

A companion volume to the popular *Christian Bed & Breakfast Directory*, this tantalizing cookbook includes the "specialties of the house" from bed and breakfast establishments across the United States and Canada. With over 500 pages of recipes such as "Breakfast in a Cookie," "Irish Soda Bread," and "Mississippi Fried Pies" featuring serving suggestions, garnishes, and the history or origin of most recipes, it's more than a bargain at $3.97.

528 pages; paperbound; 5" x 8"

Heart♥ng

CONTEMPORARY ROMANCE IS CHEAPER BY THE DOZEN!

Any 12 *Heartsong Presents* titles for only $26.95 **

Buy any assortment of twelve *Heartsong Presents* titles and save 25% off of the already discounted price of $2.95 each!

**plus $1.00 shipping and handling per order and sales tax where applicable.

HEARTSONG PRESENTS TITLES AVAILABLE NOW:

(If ordering from this page, please remember to include it with the order form.)

·········· Presents ··········

Great Inspirational Romance at a Great Price!

Heartsong Presents books are inspirational romances in contemporary and historical settings, designed to give you an enjoyable, spirit-lifting reading experience. You can choose wonderfully written titles from some of today's best authors like Veda Boyd Jones, Yvonne Lehman, Tracie J. Peterson, Nancy N. Rue, and many others.

When ordering quantities less than twelve, above titles are $2.95 each.